"Goldberg complicates things, in brilliant and moving ways, in stories that live along the border between the mundane and the surreal...Goldberg's prose is deceptively smooth, like a vanilla milkshake spiked with grain alcohol, and his ideas are always made more complex and engaging by the offbeat angles his stories take."
—*Chicago Tribune*

"A keen voice, profound insight...Each story excites on its own. Fortunate the writer who discovers his obsessions early, for he'll have that much more time to transform them in fiction, to provoke the sources of their fearsome power...*Simplify* is devilishly entertaining."
—*Los Angeles Times*

"Goldberg's best stories are told in retrospect, as if the narrators need psychic distance to fashion their memories in the most potent form."
—*Washington Post*

"Goldberg has thought a lot about the human condition and the way our hearts and minds define us. He is effortlessly brilliant with his pared-down prose and attention to detail. In a society that is disinclined to contemplate our own deaths, Goldberg hits it head-on with no qualms or fluff. His stories will provoke and startle you."
—*Bookslut*

# OTHER RESORT CITIES

# OTHER
# RESORT
# CITIES

stories

# Tod
# Goldberg

an imprint of Dzanc Books
3629 N. Hoyne
Chicago, IL 60618
www.ovbooks.org
OVBooks@aol.com

Published 2009 by Other Voices Books, an imprint of Dzanc Books
Book design by Steven Seighman
Cover photo by Ned & Shiva Productions

06 07 08 09 10 11 5 4 3 2 1
First Edition October 2009

ISBN-13: 978-0-9815899-9-2

Printed in the United States of America

# CONTENTS

For Wendy: Someday girl, I don't know when,
we're gonna get to that place...

Hold no man responsible for what he says in his grief.
— The Talmud

# The Salt

Beneath the water, beneath time, beneath yesterday, is the salt.

The paper says that another body has washed up on the north shore of the Salton Sea, its age the provenance of anthropologists. "Washed up" is a misnomer, of course, because nothing is flowing out of the Salton Sea during this winter of interminable heat: it's January 10, and the temperature hovers near one hundred degrees. The Salton Sea is receding back into memory, revealing with each inch another year, another foundation, another hand that pulls from the sand and grasps at the dead air. Maybe the bodies are from the old Indian cemetery first swallowed by the sea in 1971. Perhaps they are from Tom Sanderson's family plot. Or maybe it is my sweet Katherine, delivered back to me in rusted bone.

I fold the newspaper and set it down on my lap. Through the living room window I see Kim, my wife of seven months, pruning her roses. They are supposed to be dormant by now, she told me yesterday, and that they are alive and flowering is nothing short of a miracle. Much is miraculous to Kim: we met at the cancer treatment center in Palm Springs a little over a year ago, both of us bald and withered, our lives clinging to a chemical cocktail.

"How long did they give you?" she asked.

"Nothing specific," I said. The truth was that my doctor told me that I had a year, possibly less, but that at my age—I was seventy-two then—the script was likely to be without too many twists: I'd either live or I wouldn't. And after spending every afternoon for three months hooked to an IV, I wasn't sure if that was completely accurate. What kind of life was this that predicated itself on waiting?

"I'm already supposed to be dead," she said. "How do you like that?"

"You should buy a lottery ticket," I said.

She rummaged in her purse, pulled out a handful of stubs, and handed them to me. "Pick out one you like and if you win, we'll split it."

We live together now behind a gate in Indian Wells, and our backyard abuts a golf course that my knees won't allow me to play on and that my checkbook can't afford. My yearly pension from the Sheriff's Department more suited for the guard gate than the country club. But Kim comes from money, or at least her ex-husband did, and so here we are living out the bonus years together. At least Kim's hair has grown back.

I pick the newspaper back up and try not to read the stories on the front page, the colored bar-graph that details the Salton Sea's water levels from 1906 until present day, the old photos of speed boat races, the black bag that holds a human form, the telephone poles jutting out of the placid water, the quotes from environmentalists decrying the ecological disaster of California's fetid inland sea. I try to read page A-3, where the other big local news stories of the day are housed safely out of sight from passing tourists: *Broken Water*

*Pipe Closes Ralphs in Palm Springs. Dead Body Found in Joshua Tree Identified as Missing Hiker from Kansas. Free flu shots for Seniors at Eisenhower Medical Center.*

"Morris," Kim says. "Are you feeling all right?"

I see that Kim is standing only a few inches from me, worry etched on her face like sediment. "I'm fine," I say. "When did you come in?"

"I've been standing here talking to you, and you haven't even looked up from the paper," she says.

"I didn't hear you," I say.

"I know that," she says. "You were talking to yourself. It would be impossible for you to hear me over the din of your own conversation." Kim smiles, but I can see that she's worried.

"I'm an old man," I say.

She leans down then, takes my face in her hands, and runs her thumbs along my eyes. "You're just a boy," Kim says, and I realize she's wiping tears from my face. "Why don't you ever talk to me about your first wife? It wouldn't bother me, Morris. It would make me feel closer to you."

"That was another life," I say.

"Apparently not," she says.

"She's been gone a long time," I say, "but sometimes it just creeps back on me, and it's like she's still alive and in the other room, but I can't seem to figure out where that room is. And then I look up and my new wife is wiping tears from my face."

"I'm not your new wife," Kim says, standing back up. "I'm your last wife."

"You know what I mean," I say.

"Of course I do," Kim says.

The fact of the matter, I think after Kim has walked back outside, is that with each passing day I find my mind has begun to recede like the sea, and each morning I wake up feeling like I'm younger, like time is flowing backward, that eventually I'll open my eyes and it will be 1962 again and life will feel filled with possibility. What is obvious to me, and what my neurologist confirmed a few weeks ago, but which I haven't bothered to share with Kim, is that my brain is shedding space; that soon all that will be left is the past, my consciousness doing its best imitation of liquefaction.

I go into the bedroom and change into a pair of khaki pants, a button-down shirt, and a ball cap emblazoned with the logo of our country club. In the closet, I take down the shoe box where I keep my gun and ankle holster, and for a long time I just look at both of them, wondering what the hell I'm thinking about, what the hell I hope to prove after almost forty-five years, what exactly I think I'll find out there by the shore of that rotting sea but ghosts and sand.

Dead is still dead.

I find Kim in the front yard. She's chatting with our next-door neighbors, Sue and Leon. Last week, Leon wandered out of his house in the night and stood on the fifteenth fairway shouting obscenities. By the time I was able to coax him into my golf cart he'd stripped off all his clothes and was masturbating furiously, sadly to no avail. That's the tragedy of getting old and losing your mind—that switch flips, and everything that's been sitting limply beside you starts perking up again, but you can't figure out exactly how to work it. Today, he's smiling and happy and has a general idea about his whereabouts, but he seems blissfully unaware of who he is, or who any of us are.

"I can't thank you enough for the other night," Sue says when I walk up.

"It's nothing," I say.

"He was happy to do it," Kim says. "Any time you need help, really, we're just right here."

"His medication . . . Well, you know how it is. You have to get it regulated. I wish you'd known him before all of this," Sue says, waving her hands dismissively, and then, just like that, she's sobbing. "Oh, it's silly. We get old, don't we, Kim? We just get old, and next thing you know, you're gone."

Leon used to run some Fortune 500 company that made light fixtures for casinos. They called him The King of Lights, or at least that's what he told me once in one of his more lucid moments. But today he's just a dim bulb, and I can't help but think of how soon I'll be sitting right there next to him at the loony bin, drooling on myself and letting some orderly wipe my ass.

"I have to run out," I say to Kim, once Leon and Sue have made their way back to their condo.

"I could clean up and come with you," she says. "It would just take a moment."

"Don't bother," I say. "I'm just gonna drive on out to the Salton Sea. See what's going on down there. Talk a little cop shop."

"Morris," she says. "If I go inside and look in the closet, will I find your gun there?"

"I'm afraid not," I say.

"You're a fool to be running around with that thing. Do you hear me?"

We stand there staring at each other for a solid minute until Kim shakes her head once, turns heel, and walks inside. She doesn't bother to slam the front door, which makes it worse.

In the spring of 1962, I took a job working for Claxson Oil and moved, along with my young wife Katherine, to the Salton Sea. Claxson had hired me to be the de facto police for the five hundred people they'd shipped into the area in their attempt to find oil beneath the sea, a venture that would prove fruitless and tragic. At the time, though, Claxson was simply concerned about keeping order: they'd already built an army-style barracks and were busy constructing seafront hacienda homes for the executives who'd oversee the dig and, presumably, the boomtown that would come once the oil came spouting out of the ground. My job was to provide a little bit of law, both with the working men (and families) and the Mexicans and Indians who populated the area. There'd already been three stabbing deaths in the past year—two roughnecks and one Mexican—and it didn't seem to be getting better.

I was only twenty-eight years old then and had spent the previous three years trying to figure out how to get Korea out of my head. I served two years in Korea during the war and another five trying to conjure a better future for myself by reenlisting until it seemed pointless, before finally returning to Granite City, Washington, where I'd grown up. My father was the sheriff there—as I would later be—so he hired me on to be his deputy. It was reasonable work until a young woman named Gretchen Claxson went missing from the small fishing resort on Granite Lake. I found her body, and the man who'd done unspeakable things to it, a few sleepless weeks later. I'd like to say that I was honest and fair with the killer, a man named Milton Stairs who I'd gone to elementary school with, but the truth is that I nearly killed him: I broke both of his arms and beat him so badly that he ended up losing the ability to speak. I was rewarded with a job offer from Gretchen's grieving oil baron father and a salary well beyond my comprehension.

A year and a half later, Katherine would be dead from ovarian cancer and I'd be back in Granite City.

But today I'm standing on the other side of a stretch of yellow caution tape, though this isn't a crime scene, watching as a rental security officer stands guard over a patch of dirt while two young women and a man wearing one of those safari vests brush rocks and debris away from a depression in the earth. The Salton Sea laps at the edge of the sand, the stench rising from it as thick as mustard gas. The two women and the man are all wearing masks, but the security guard just keeps a handkerchief to his face while in the other hand he clutches a clipboard. It's not the body that smells—it's the sea, rotting with dead fish, sewage runoff, and the aroma of red tide algae.

Forty years ago, this was roughly where Bonnie Livingston had her little bar and café. At night during the week, the working men would sit at the bar drinking the stink out of their skin, but on the weekends the LA people would drive in with their boats and water skis and, eventually, speedboats, and would come into Bonnie's looking for authenticity. More often than not, they'd leave without a few teeth and, on occasion, without their girlfriends, wives, or daughters. They thought the Salt would be like an inland Riviera. They thought we'd find oil and prosperity, and that a city would rise from the fetid desert floor.

Thirty-eight years ago, Bonnie's bar slipped into the sea. Thirty-five years ago, Bonnie's home followed suit. Shortly thereafter Bonnie followed her bar and house, simply walking into the water with a bottle of wine in her hand, drinking big gulps all along the way. They never did find her body, but that was okay: her entire family watched her walk into the sea, bricks tied around her ankles. It wasn't a suicide, her son wrote to tell me, because she'd been dead for at least three years, but more a celebration of the Salt. All things return to it.

At some point, however, memory becomes insufficient in the face of commerce and space. These bodies that keep pulling themselves from the sea are a hindrance to something larger and more important than an old man's past: real estate. The Chuyalla Indians intend to put a twenty-six-floor hotel and casino here, and then, in five years, one hundred condos. They intend to fund a project that will eradicate the dead—both the people and the lingering fumes of a sea that was never meant to be—and once again tempt the folly of beachside living in the middle of the desert.

I'll be dead by then myself. Or at least without the ability to know the difference.

The security guard finally notices me and ambles over, his gait slow and deliberate, as if traversing the twenty feet from the body to the tape were the most difficult task of his life. "Can I help you?" he asks, not bothering to remove the handkerchief from his face. I'd guess that he's just a shade under sixty himself, too old for real police work, which probably makes this the perfect job for him.

"Just came down to see the excitement," I say. I open my wallet and show him my retired sheriff's card. He looks at it once, nods, and then from out of his back pocket he fishes out his own wallet and shows me *his* retirement card from the Yuma, Arizona PD. His name is Ted Farmer he tells me, and then he explains, as former cops are apt to do, the exact path he took from being a real cop to a rental cop. When he runs out of story, he turns his attention back to the body in the sand.

"Yep," he says, motioning his head in the direction of the grave. "Lotta fireworks. My opinion? They should just leave the bodies where they are. No point digging them up just to move them somewhere else." One of the female anthropologists carries a hand and wrist over to a white plastic sheet and sets them down across from another hand and wrist. "That first hand? Still had rings on it. That sorta thing messes with your head. It's dumb, I know. Lady's probably been dead fifty, a hundred years, more fertilizer than person. But still."

About two hundred yards from the shore a small aluminum boat with a screaming outboard motor trolls back and forth. I can just make out the outline of a shirtless man sitting at one end, a little boy at the other, a long fishing pole bent between them. When she was at her sickest, when it was apparent that the only salve for her illness was the belief that tomorrow could only be better, when we'd begun to live in increments, separating the positives into single grains of sand, Katherine was certain that when she was well (never if) we'd have a houseboat on this inland sea, that our lives would be lived rarely touching land, that each morning we'd pick up anchor and find another destination, another view of the sun-charred Chocolate Mountains.

When she passed, I gave her that.

I look now at the bones being sluiced from the ground and know, of course, that it's not Katherine. Oh, but she is here, holding my hand as we walk from Bonnie's and dip our toes into the water, the air alive with laughter behind us, music wafting through the thick summer air, Chuck Berry singing "Johnny B. Goode" into eternity. Her hair is pulled back from her face and she's wearing a V-neck white T-shirt, her tanned skin darkening the fabric just slightly, a scent of vanilla lifting from her skin. It's 1962. It's 1963. It's today or it's yesterday or it's tomorrow.

"You okay, pal?" Farmer says. I look down and see that he's got a hand on my chest, steadying me. "Drifting a bit to stern there."

"Not used to the heat anymore," I say, though the truth is that I feel fine. Though my perception is dipping sideways, it does not bother me. Seeing the past like a ghost is a welcome part of my new condition, and if it brings with it a few disorienting side effects, I suppose I'm willing to make the trade. Farmer fetches me an unused bucket from aside the dig, turns it over, and directs me to sit. After the horizon has straightened out, I say, "I used to be the law out here, if you can believe that."

"When was that?"

"About a million years ago," I say. "Or it could have been fifteen minutes ago."

Farmer winces noticeably, like he knows what I mean. We watch the anthropologists going about their work in silence. It becomes clear after a while that the two young women are actually students—graduate students, most likely—and that the man in the funny vest is the professor. Every few minutes he gathers their attention and explains something pertaining to what they've found. At one point, he goes back to the white plastic sheet and lifts up a leg they've pried from the earth and makes sure his students have made note of an abnormality in the femur, a dent of some kind.

"You know what I think?" Farmer says. "Guys like us, we've seen too much crazy shit, our brains don't have enough room to keep it all. Pretty soon it just starts leaking out."

"You're probably right," I say.

"I guess I've seen over a hundred dead bodies," he says. "Not like this here, but like people who were alive ten minutes before I got to them. Traffic accidents and such. Sometimes I'd get called out on a murder, but I was mostly a low-hanging fruit cop, if you know what I mean. I tell you, there's something about the energy surrounding a dead body, you know? Like a dog, it can just walk by, take a sniff and keep going. Us, we got all that empathy. What I wouldn't give to lack empathy."

The two women lift the trunk of the body up out of the dirt. There's still bits of fabric stuck to the ribcage and my first thought is of those old pirate books I used to read as a kid, where the hero would find himself on a deserted island with just the clothed skeletons of previous plunderers lining the beach. How old was I when I read those books? Eight? Nine? I can still see my father sitting on the edge of my bed while I read aloud to him, how the dim light on my bedside table would cast a slicing shadow across his face, so that all I could make out was his profile. He was already a sheriff then himself, already knew about empathy, had spent a few sleepless nights on the beginnings and endings of people he'd never know, though he was only twenty-eight or twenty-nine himself. Thirty-five years he's been gone. You never stop being somebody's child, even when you can see the end of the long thread yourself. Maybe that's really what Kim finds absent; it's not simply Katherine who calls to me in the night, even when the night is as bright as day, it's all those I've lost: my father, my mother, my brother Jack, who passed before I was even born, but whose presence I was always aware of, as if I lived a life for him, too. My second wife, Margaret, and the children we never managed to have before she, too, passed. How many friends of mine are gone? All of them, even if they are still alive. And here, in the winter soil of the Salton Sea, the air buttressed by an ungodly heat, I remember the ghosts of another life, still. These bodies that keep appearing could be mine; if not my responsibility, my knowledge, my own real estate.

I tell myself it's just land. My mind has ascribed emotion to a mere parcel of a planet. It's the very duplicity of existence that plays with an old man's mind, particularly when you can see regret in a tangible form alongside the spectral one that visits periodically.

"They bother looking for kin?" I ask.

"Oh, sure," Farmer says. He waves his clipboard and for the first time I notice that it's lined with names and dates and addresses. "We got some old records from back when Claxson was out here, detailing where a few family plots are and such. Claxson kept pretty good records of who came and went, but this place has flooded and receded so many times, you can't be sure where these bodies are from. Back then, people died they just dug a hole and slid them in, seems like."

"That's about right," I say.

"Anyway, we get a couple visitors a week, like yourself."

"I'm just out for a drive," I say.

"What did you say your name was?"

"Morris Drew," I say.

Farmer flips a few pages, running his finger down the lines of names, and then pauses. "I'm sorry," he says quietly.

"So am I," I say.

I drive south along the beaten access road that used to run behind the marina but now is covered in ruts and divots, the pavement long since cracked and weathered away, plant life and shrubs growing between bits of blacktop. Back when Claxson Oil still believed life could take place here, they built the infrastructure to sustain a population of one hundred thousand, so beneath the desert floor there's plumbing and power lines waiting to be used, a city of coils and pipes to carry subsistence to a casino, one hundred condominiums, tourists from Japan. They'll bring in alien vegetation to gussy up the desert, just as they have outside my home on the twelfth hole; they'll install sprinklers to wash away the detritus of fifty years of emptiness. There are maybe six hundred people living permanently around the Salton Sea, Ted Farmer told me—more if you count the meth addicts and Vietnam and Gulf War vets out in Slab City, the former Air Force base that became a squatter's paradise.

I stop my car when I see the shell of the old Claxson barracks rising up a few hundred yards in the distance. To the east, a flock of egrets has landed on the sea, their slim bodies undulating in the water just beyond the shoreline. They've flown south for the winter but probably didn't realize they'd land in the summer. I can make out the noise from the lone boat on the water.

The barracks themselves are a Swiss cheese of mortar and drywall, to the point that even from this distance I can see the sparse traffic on Highway 80 through its walls, as if a newsreel from the future has been projected onto the past. Farmer warned me not to go into the old building— that transients, drug addicts, and illegals frequently use it for scavenging and business purposes.

It's not the barracks that I'm interested in; they merely provide a map for my memory, a placeholder for a vision that blinds me with its radiance. It's 1962 and I'm parked in my new Corvair, Katherine by my side, and we're scanning the scrub for the view she wants. It's not the topography that she cares about; it's the angle of the sun. She tells me that anyone can have a view of the mountains, anyone can have a view of the sea, but after living in the Pacific Northwest her entire life, she desires a view of the sun. Katherine wanted a morning room that would be flooded in natural light at dawn, that would be dappled in long shadows in the afternoon, that at night would glow white from the moon. "All my life I've lived in clouds," she said. "I think I deserve a view of the sun." She got out of the Corvair right about *here*, I think, and she walked out into the desert, striding through the tangles of brush and sand while I watched her from the front seat. She was so terribly young, just twenty-three, but I know she felt like she'd already lived a good portion of her life out, that she needed to be a *woman* and not the girl she was. She always told me that she envied the experiences I'd had already in life, that she wished she could see Asia as I had, wished that she knew what it felt like to hold a gun with malice, because to her that was the thing about me that was most unknowable.

Late at night, she'd wake me and ask me what it felt like to kill someone, to know that there was another family, somewhere in North Korea, that didn't have a father. She didn't ask this in anger, she said, only that it was the sort of thing that kept her awake at night, knowing that the man sleeping beside her, the man she loved, had killed before. I'd see Katherine get old before time had found its bearing with her, long before she was done being a girl. I would see her bald and shapeless, her bones the density of straw. I would hear her beg for me to use my gun without malice, to save her from the suffering of her very body, to relieve the pressure that boiled through her skin, the slow withering of her veins, the viscous loss of self that would turn her into something foreign and angry, her voice the consistency of withered crabgrass, begging me, begging me, pleading for a mechanical end to an unnatural death sentence. I would see her in the moonlit glow of the Salton Sea, her body slipping between my hands into the deep, murky waters.

I step out of the car and see Katherine, her face turned to the sun, motioning for me to join her, to see what she sees. She calls out for me to hurry, to join her there in the spot that will be our home. Did this happen? I'm not sure anymore, but at this moment it is true. Surrounding me are nearly a dozen old foundations, this tract of desert bifurcated by the phantom remains of paved roads and cul-de-sacs. From above, I imagine the land surrounding the old barracks must look like a petroglyph left by an ancient civilization.

I triangulate myself with the sea, the mountain, and the barracks and then close my eyes and walk forward, allowing my sense memory to guide me, to find the cement that was my home. But it's useless: I trip over a tumbleweed and nearly fall face first onto the ground. Sweet Christ, I think, it's lucky I didn't break my hip! How long would it be before anyone found me? With the heat as it is, I'd die from exposure before Kim even noticed that we'd missed the early bird at Sherman's Deli. So instead I walk from foundation to foundation, hoping that the layout of the Claxson Oil Executive Housing Unit makes itself clear. I picture the payroll manager, Gifford Lewis, and his wife, Lois, sitting on their patio drinking lemonade, their baby frolicking between them in a playpen. I picture Jeff Morton, sitting in his backyard, strumming a guitar he didn't know how to play. I picture Sassy, the Jefferies' cocker spaniel, running across the street to our scratch of grass, her tail wagging in a furious motion. I picture myself leaning down to pet Sassy and the way the dog would lick up the length of my arm, her tongue rough and dry from the heat and how I would step inside and get a water bowl for the dog, and that the dog would sit and wait patiently for my return and then would lap up the water in a fuss, drops flying from the bowl and catching hits of sun so that each drop glimmered a brilliant white.

I try to see the world as it was and as it is now, try to find what used to be my home, what used to be my life, try to locate the Fourth Estate of my memory: a dry reporting of fact. You lived *here*. You slept *there*. You made love and you witnessed death and you mourned and you buried your wife in the simple plot Claxson provided and allowed behind your home and you carried your wife's corpse—because that's what it was; it wasn't a body anymore, not with the dirt and the sand and absence of any kind of reality, any kind of relevance beyond what you'd emotionally ascribed to it—to the sea, because that was what she asked of you, not to allow her to rot in the desert, but to give her a perpetual view of the sun and the water, to let her float free of the pain, because that's what she wanted you to give her. That is *across the way*. And you see the end of your own life, don't you? You feel the creeping dread that you've beaten that same slow poison yourself but have found another, more insidious invader. And what will you do about it, Morris Drew? Why did you bring that gun with you?

When I get back home I find Kim sitting on our back patio, her eyes buried in a magazine, golf carts moving in a steady stream past her as dusk has begun to fall. She doesn't see me, so for a time I just stare at her. I imagine what she might look like with the fine lines around her eyes smooth, her gray hair blond, her skin thick and healthy instead of thin and stretched like parchment. The trauma of memory is that it never forgives you for aging. What would Katherine look like to me today? Would she be an old woman, or would she be young in my eyes, perpetually twenty three years old? The other trauma of memory is that it can absolve you of reality if you let it, and the reality is that I've come to love other women, finally, a fact I'm not ashamed of.

"I'm home," I say.

"I know," Kim says, not looking up.

"I didn't know if you heard me come in," I say.

"Morris," she says, turning pages, "your footfalls have the delicacy of a jackhammer. There are no secrets between tile floors and you."

I sit down beside Kim and put my arm around her and pull her close. I see the young woman she must have been. I've seen photos, of course, but you never truly see someone in a photo. You see what they looked like, but not who they were. Fear shows you all the colors in a person's skin.

I reach down and lift up my pant leg and show her my empty holster. "I almost killed myself today. I'm not proud of that, but I wanted you to know that it won't happen again."

"Jesus, Morris," she says.

"I threw that gun into the Salton Sea," I say. "Even said some prayers over it. I'm not gonna let it take me from you."

I know that if I look down I'll find Kim crying, so I stare instead at the long shadows crawling into the bunkers on either side of the twelfth hole, at the last glimmers of sunlight that peek over the rim of the San Jacinto Mountains, at the green shards of grass that grow just beyond our patio. I watch as lights flicker on inside the condos across the fairway from us, and I think that where I am now, at this very moment, with my wife beside me, with a hint of cool in the breeze that has swept by me, the smell of jasmine light on its trail, *this* is the memory I want to live out the rest of my years with. A moment of silent perfection when I knew, finally knew, that I'd found a kind of contentment with who I was, who I'd been, and what I'd tried so desperately to forget. I am not surprised, then, when a strong gust of wind picks up from the east and I make out the faint scent of the Salton Sea, pungent and lost and so far, far away.

# Mitzvah

**T**hat Rabbi David Cohen wasn't Jewish had ceased, over time, to be a problem. He hardly even thought of it anymore except when ordering breakfast down at the Bagel Café. He'd sit there across from Bennie Savone, that fat fuck, watching him wolf down ham and scrambled eggs, or French toast with a steaming side of greasy link sausage, and his mouth would actually start to water, like he was some kind of fucking golden retriever. He didn't even think Bennie liked pork all that much—sometimes Bennie would order a cup of coffee and a side of bacon and would leave the bacon uneaten, David assumed, in not-so-benign mockery—but David knew Bennie liked letting him know who was in control of the situation.

But now, as he sat in his normal booth in the back corner facing the busy intersection of Buffalo and Westcliff, waiting for Bennie to roll up in his absurd black Mercedes that might as well have a personalized plate that said MOBSTER on it, he thought that he probably qualified as a Jew by now, if not in the eyes of God, then at least in his own eyes. It still wasn't that he gave a fuck about religion—his personal motto, before all of this shit, had been "everybody dies"—but he probably knew far more about the Torah and the culture in general than the people who belonged to the Temple. And had he grown up with it, David was fairly certain he would have appreciated the subtle nuance of kugel.

After fifteen years, though, he still couldn't get used to the idea of baked noodles, raisins, apples, and cinnamon as a fucking entrée. Now pork loin. Pork loin was something he could get behind, especially this time of year, what with Christmas coming up. Back in the day, his wife Jennifer knew how to make it just how he liked. Brined in salt overnight, covered with juniper berries, a bit of garlic, maybe some thyme, and then slow roasted for three hours, until even the garage smelled like it.

Christ.

Fifteen fucking years and for what? He understood that his situation was fairly untenable these days, that those fucking Muslims had changed the way Family business was handled, particularly as it related to guys like David whose fake paperwork was fine in a company town like Las Vegas but wouldn't pass muster even in Reno. David wasn't inclined to give too much thought to the whole Israel-Palestine issue, but he had to keep abreast of shit in case someone dared ask his opinion, though he never could confide in anyone that he shared some anger issues with the Palestinians at least as it related to real estate, confined as he was to Las Vegas.

"Can I get you something, Rabbi?"

David looked up from his reverie and saw the smiling face of Shoshana Goldblatt. Her parents, Stan and Alta, were two of the biggest donors Temple Beth Israel had, and yet here she was busting her ass on a Tuesday morning running tables. And that was an ass, David had to admit. She was only eighteen and he'd known her since she was five, but . . . damn.

"A cup of coffee would be fine, Shoshana," David said. "I'm waiting on Mr. Savone, as usual, so maybe just a toasted onion bagel for now."

Shoshana took down his order, but he could tell that something was bothering the girl. It was the way it took her nearly an entire minute to write the words "coffee" and "bagel" on her pad, her eyes welling up with tears the entire time. It was always like this. He'd go somewhere to just chill out, maybe smoke a cigar and catch a ballgame over at J.C. Wooloughan's pub, and next thing he knew one of his fucking Israelites would pull up next to him with some metaphysical calamity.

"Is there something wrong, Shoshana?" he asked. When she slid into the booth across from him and deposited her head into her hands, thick phlegmy sobs spilling out of that beautiful mouth he'd just sort of imagined his dick in, he felt himself wince and hoped she didn't notice. He'd spent the better part of his life avoiding crying women of all ages, never really knowing what to say to them other than "Shut the fuck up, you stupid whore," and that hadn't seemed to help anyone, least of all himself. Whatever was wrong with Shoshana Goldblatt would invariably ruin David's whole fucking day. First there'd be the guilt he felt hearing her secrets, and then there'd be the guilt associated with him finding it all rather humorous.

"Oh, Rabbi," she said. "I wanted to just come in and talk to you in private, but there's always such a crowd, and my mom, you know, she's always telling me to not bother you with my problems, that you're a busy man and all, so I'm like, okay, I'll just figure it out for myself, but then, like, you're always saying that we should trust that the Torah has answers to all of our problems, right?"

"That's right, Shoshana," he said, though he wasn't sure if he'd ever said such a thing. Most of the time, he just downloaded shit off the Internet now, but it seemed plausible that at some point he said something like that.

"I'm just so confused," she said, before explaining to David a scenario that involved, as best as David could suss out, her having sex with three different black guys from the UNLV basketball team while a graduate assistant coach filmed the whole thing on his camera phone. It was hard for David to concentrate completely on the story since Bennie Savone had entered the restaurant about five minutes in and was stalking angrily about the bakery area, dragging his black attaché case against the pastry windows, like he was banging his cup against the prison bars. So when David sensed that Shoshana had come to the basic conclusion of the issue—that she'd liked it, that she wondered what was wrong with her, but that she wanted to do it again, and with more guys—he reached across the table and took both of her hands in his.

"There's a part of the Midrash that says, essentially, we are all allowed to find enjoyment in the company of others," David said. He'd found that if he simply dropped the Midrash into conversation, rejoined with the word "essentially," and then paraphrased Neil Young or Bruce Springsteen, people left him feeling like they'd learned something. It was true that he knew a few things from the Midrash, had even read a great deal of it, but, in dealing with an eighteen-year-old girl just learning the joys of a filmed gangbang, he didn't feel the need to reach too deep. "Is a dream a lie if it doesn't come true, Shoshana? Of course not. It's something far, far worse. Do you understand?"

He let go of the girl's hands then and handed her the handkerchief from the breast pocket of his sport coat. She wiped her eyes, blew her nose, and smiled wanly at David, though now he couldn't even look her in the eye. "Thank you so much, Rabbi Cohen. I think I see that path now," she said and slid out of the booth, not even bothering to return his hanky to him.

Bennie, unfortunately, took her spot. "Fuck's wrong with her?"

"Confused about love," David said.

Bennie nodded. "Who isn't?"

It was weird. Over the course of their rather unconventional business relationship, Bennie Savone had found it necessary to use David as his father confessor, too, even though he knew that Rabbi David Cohen was previously Sal Cupertine; that before he was a fake rabbi, he was a Chicago "associate" who'd accidentally killed three undercover Donnie Brasco motherfuckers on the same botched contract, and that, barring a sudden religious experience the likes of which only happened in prison movies, David's moral center was still pretty opaque. Still, David reasoned that Bennie needed to talk to someone, particularly since the one person Bennie could depend on previously had been the rabbi David replaced three years ago, Rabbi Ronald Kales, who also happened to be Bennie's father-in-law . . . or was, until that unfortunate "boating accident" on Lake Meade claimed his life.

David knew that Bennie's decision not to fish out of the same shallow, polluted pond of local and loyal Italian women or coke-whore strippers most of his friends and co-workers had, opting instead to get connected with the real

Las Vegas money—the Summerlin Jews—was still a source of some lingering organizational shame; an issue David was certainly intimate with.

"Yes, well," David said. "She's still young."

"My daughter tells me Shoshana likes black guys," Bennie says.

Sometimes David tried to imagine what his life would be like if he were still in Chicago, but he'd somehow had a different kind of upbringing, so that now he was selling real estate on the North Shore or running a sports bar or deli or was just a fucking Culligan Man, his ends meeting, his life happy. Would he still end up on Tuesday mornings gossiping about whom eighteen-year-old girls were or were not fucking?

"I have to prepare for a talk at the Senior Center this afternoon," David said, "so I'm afraid I don't have much time to chat. Can we get down to business?"

"Of course, Rabbi," Bennie said. "I'd hate to get in the way of your busy schedule of dick and ribbon cuttings." Bennie reached into his attaché and pulled out a manila envelope and slid it across the table. "You got a funeral on Thursday and one coming up next week, too. Maybe two. Have to see how that one shakes out. Got a very sick relative. Could go anytime."

David just nodded. The holidays tended to be Bennie's busy season with murder, and now that they were flying bodies (or at least parts of them) in on private jets periodically from Chicago or driving them up from Los Angeles, David expected the news. Plus, David sort of marveled at Bennie's ingenuity; the guy seemed like a dumb crook from the outside, but on the inside Bennie had a real aptitude for business. Stan and Alta Goldblatt might have been big donors, but Bennie Savone, with his Jewish wife and three Jewish children, was like fucking UNICEF to Temple Beth Israel. He single-handedly financed the building of Summerlin's first Jewish mortuary and cemetery behind the Temple's expansive campus on Hillpointe, championed the new high school that was breaking ground in the spring, and, of course, regularly met with the Temple's esteemed rabbi over at the Bagel Café to discuss the livelihood of the Jewish faith (or whatever the fuck that shit rag mob columnist John L. Smith in the *Review-Journal* said in one of his weekly innuendo-fests. If David ever had the desire to start killing people again, he'd start with that hack) and issues related to the regular laundering of over fifteen million dollars every year through the Temple's coffers. David imagined that Bennie's long-range foresight could help a lot of Fortune 500 companies—it's not like any other mobsters had the fucking chutzpah to bury their enemies and war dead in a cemetery, nor the willingness to put all the pieces in place years before they'd even see them in action. That Bennie earned most of his living from strip clubs didn't bother anyone at the Temple. That's where everyone did business anyway.

"Fine," David said. "Anything else?"

"Yeah," Bennie said. "My wife wants to know what your Hanukkah plans are this year."

"I'll be staying home," David said, though the truth was that at least half the time would be spent at the Temple making sure the young rabbi he'd entrusted with most of the social activities didn't burn the fucking place down, literally. That kid was a menace around an open flame.

"You know you got an open invitation," Bennie said. "Come over all eight nights. Spin the fucking dreidel. Eat fucking pancakes. Listen to Neil Diamond sing 'Rudolph the Red Nosed Reindeer.' You like Neil Diamond, right, Rabbi?"

What David really wanted, more than anything, was to get up from the booth, climb into his Range Rover, and drive it into a brick wall, just to feel something authentic again, even if it was pain. "The Jewish Sinatra," David said.

Shoshana brought David his bagel and coffee and discreetly set his hanky back down on the table. He looked up at her and she seemed . . . happy. Like she'd had a tremendous weight lifted from her shoulders and now could go on living her life in perfect happiness, her every orifice filled with big black cock. David felt something shift in his bowels; something he thought might be his conscience picking up enema speed.

"Listen," David said quietly after Shoshana left. "I gotta get out of here. A vacation. Something. I'm about to lose my mind. Promise me, after Christmas, you'll look at this situation. It's been fifteen years, Benjamin." He said Bennie's full first name just to piss him off a little. "You realize I haven't even left the *city limits* since 9/11?"

"Yeah, yeah," Bennie said, "sure. Talk to me again after the holidays. We'll see what we can do. Don't want you getting soft . . . Sally."

Rabbi David Cohen looked out the window again and wondered how it was he was the only fucking person who *happened* in Vegas and now had to fucking stay in Vegas. Put his old mug shot on a tourist brochure then see how many people kept visiting.

When David first came to Las Vegas in 1993—back when he was still Sal Cupertine—he couldn't get over how wide open the desert was, how at night, if you weren't on the Strip or downtown, the sky seemed to stretch for miles unimpeded. At dusk, Red Rock Canyon would glow golden with strands of dying sunlight, and he'd imagine what his wife, Jennifer, would have made of the vision. She was always taking art classes at the community college in Chicago, though never with much success, but he thought then that if she were with him in Las Vegas and tried to paint the sunset, well, he'd pretend to love her interpretation. Used to be pretending was hard work. He was only thirty-five when he got to Las Vegas, but still felt seventeen, which meant he wasn't scared of anyone and didn't give a damn if he hurt people's feelings. It was a good skill set for his previous line of work, but David had long ago concluded it was shit on his interpersonal relationships. And the irony, of course, was that now all he ever did anymore was pretend while listening to people's problems. David was inclined to believe that his adopted religion was right about heaven and hell being a place on Earth.

It was four o'clock on Wednesday, and David was already late for a meeting at the Temple about next year's Jewish Book Fair, but he couldn't seem to shake the feeling that the previous morning's conversation with Shoshana, and the one directly following it with Bennie, had somehow clarified a few things that had been gnawing at his mind the last several weeks. So instead of attending the meeting, he drove his Temple-purchased Range Rover the four blocks from his Temple-purchased home on the fifteenth hole at TPC over to Bruce Trent Park, where he wandered among the stalls being set up for the Farmer's Market and tried to line up his priorities.

He stopped and smelled some apples, made idle talk about funnel cakes with the Mexican girl fixing them over what looked like a Bunsen burner, watched children fling themselves over and under the monkey bars. If he closed his eyes and just focused on what he could hear and smell, it was almost like he was back in Chicago, though by now the sounds and smells tended to mostly remind him of his first days in Las Vegas when he spent all of his time foolishly searching for things that reminded him of home. It had grown increasingly difficult for David to even conjure *that* memory accurately, since the landscape, both mental and physical, had changed so drastically in the intervening years. Where there used to be open vistas, the Howard Hughes Corporation had built the master-planned community of Summerlin, filling in the desert with thousands of houses, absurd traffic circles instead of stop signs, acres of green grass, and the commerce such development demanded: looming casinos that eroded his favorite mountain views, Target after Target, a Starbucks every thirty paces, and shopping centers anchored on one corner by a Smith's and on the other by some bar that was just a video poker machine with a roof.

But something about today seemed to cloak everything in radiance. Orthodox Jews tended to talk about such things as if they were moments of vast spiritual enlightenment, though David tended to think the Orthodox Jews were a little on the fruity side of things—always dropping Ezekiel's vision of the Valley of Bones like that guy wasn't a fucking whack job of the first order—so it was a good thing Temple Beth Israel was reform, which meant David just had to know some of that hocus-pocus shit, but didn't have to talk about it too much and certainly didn't have to dress in that stupid black getup. Still, his mind felt clear today, and whether it was a religious experience or just the settling of some internal debts didn't particularly vex David, because the result was the same: chiefly, that he knew he needed to get the fuck out of Las Vegas before he killed himself and took twenty or thirty motherfuckers with him in the process.

That his life had become a suffocation of ironics didn't bother him. No, it was the realization that in just three weeks he'd turn fifty, and yet he constantly waited for his front door to be kicked in by U.S. Marshals; that he wasn't some dumb punk anymore who could just live his life in blindness while other people controlled his exterior life; and that, well, he missed his wife more and more with each passing moment.

The Savone family had been good to him, he couldn't deny that. They'd set him up in this life when they could have scattered him over the Midwest one tendon at a time—even had Rabbi Kales privately tutor him for two years before he started this long con, first as an assistant at the Temple's Children's Center (where he actually had responsibilities for the first time in his life), and then, steadily, they pushed him up through the Temple's ranks until, when it became clear that Rabbi Kales's old age and inability to shut the fuck up had become a liability, he ascended to the top spot.

He had a beautiful home. A beautiful car. If he needed a woman, Bennie took care of that, too. The problem was that the world around him was changing. Locally, only Bennie knew he was a fake anymore, all the other players having gone down in a fit of meshugass over at the WildHorse strip club that left a tourist dead and another one without the ability to speak. Eventually, Bennie would end up getting busted on some RICO shit (or, praise be, Bennie's wife Rachel would get a fucking sliver of conscience and/or retrospect and would roll on that fat fuck), and then one morning David would wake up and the U.S. Marshals would shove a big hook in his mouth and dangle him all over the press, the big fish that got away finally on the line.

And then there was the paralyzing issue of technology. When the Savone family moved him out of Chicago after the fuck-up, he had to leave everything behind, including his wife, Jennifer, and his infant son, William. At first, it was easy to keep them out of his mind—it was either forget them or get the death penalty, which would probably be meted out by about fifteen cops in a very small cell. But as time went on and his life became a mundane series of mornings spent holding babies' bloody dicks, brunch meetings filled with whiny plasticized rich bitches who couldn't decide which charity should get the glory of their attention, afternoons spent in pink and yellow polo shirts as he golfed with men who would have fucking spit on him in Chicago, and nights spent alone in his Ethan Allen-showroom living room, flipping channels, jerking off to Cinemax, thinking about disappearing, just getting the fuck out, moving to Mexico, or Canada, or even Los Angeles, he began paving roads toward Jennifer and William.

It was so easy: he just typed their names into Google and came up with William's MySpace page. William was seventeen now and, if his pictures were any judge, was in desperate need of some guidance. Every single picture, his fucking pants were halfway down his ass, he was throwing some fucking gang sign that actually spelled out MOB, and he had a Yankees cap—a fucking Yankees cap!—turned sideways on his head, which made him look like a fucking retard, though not unlike half the kids David saw Saturdays at the Temple. He only saw Jennifer in the background of a few photos, and it broke his heart to see how old she'd become, how her straight blond hair was now silver, how her body had grown frumpy. Time and pressure had turned her into an old woman while he was busy fucking strippers and running a goddamned Jewish empire in the middle of the desert.

But she was there. He could see her. She existed. He checked the archives of the *Tribune* and *Sun-Times* to see if her name had been in any marriage announcements but came up empty. David knew that didn't mean anything concrete, but he also thought that if she had remarried, William wouldn't have turned into such a fucking putz.

Over the last several months, he'd started looking at Google satellite photos of his old house (where, according to a simple public record search, Jennifer and William still lived). Though all he could really see was the roof and the general outline of the house, he could make out bits of himself, too: the pool, which he'd purchased after he got paid for his first substantial hit (a guy he ran track with in high school, Gil Williams, whose father was city councilman); the towering blue ash tree in the front yard, where he hung a tire swing for William; the brick driveway, Jennifer's dream, which he laid brick by brick over the course of a long weekend. Before he understood that the photos were static and not updated regularly, David would return each day to refresh the image, hoping to catch a glimpse of his wife, who he was sure he could recognize even from outer space.

Did she know he was still alive? Did she spend nights searching for him, too? Did she know he'd turned gray, too, but that he'd stayed in shape all of these years, working out, still hitting the heavy bag at the gym when he could, keeping himself ready, just in case—knowing, waiting, thinking that eventually, if he had to, he could kill someone with his hands again, just like in the day. Happy with the thought. Thinking, yesterday: *You think I'm soft? I could shove that attaché case up your ass, Bennie.* And now. Now. When would things ever be tenable if they weren't now? Life, David realized, had reached a terminal point. Years ago, Rabbi Kales explained to David that when the end of days came, the Jews would be resurrected into a perfect state and the whole of the world would take on the status of Israel, and the Jews, he told him, would live in peace there. "What about me?" David had asked then, and Rabbi Kales just shook his head and said that he'd likely just rot in the ground, right beside him probably, in light of the experience they were embroiled in. He laughed when he said it, but David was pretty sure he meant it. Well, fuck that, David thought now. It was time to get tenable.

David purchased a small bundle of sweet smelling incense from a hippie-looking girl with a barbell through her tongue. He'd seen this girl before—maybe fifty times, actually, since he was pretty sure she'd been there every single time he'd visited the Farmer's Market—but had never bothered to really notice her apart from the fact that she always stood there placidly selling fucking incense. What kind of life was that? Selling smell. She smiled sweetly at him, and David wondered how much kids today knew about the fucking world, about how things really *were*, how it wasn't all just iPods and

MySpace and throwing gang signs on the Internet, that there was something permanent about the decisions being made around them. Ramifications. Spiritual and physical. If kids wanted to know what it meant to be tough, they'd take a look at the Torah, see how the Jews rolled, see how revenge and power were really exerted. David liked thinking about the Jews as Chosen People, liked thinking that maybe, after all these years, he'd been chosen, too. You wander the desert for forty years—or just fifteen—you begin to change your perspective on things, begin to appreciate what you had before you got lost, begin to see signs, warnings, omens. Not everything was so obvious. Not everything had to be digitized to be real. Sometimes, man, you had to look inside of things.

"Let me ask you a question," David said to the girl with the pierced tongue. "Do you know me?"

"Am I supposed to?"

When he was young, he liked a girl with a little sass, but now it just annoyed him. "You see me here every week."

She shrugged. "If you say so."

"What do you think I do for a living?"

"Is this some sort of market research bullshit?"

Rabbi David Cohen—who, for thirty-five years had been a guy named Sal Cupertine, who used to like to hurt people just for the hell of it, who killed three cops and really didn't think about that at all, never even really considered it, not even after they did an episode of *Cold Case* about it that he caught one night as he was drifting off to sleep after a long wedding at Temple Beth Israel—leaned across the small table and stared into the girl's face. "I look like a market researcher to you?"

"Everyone in Vegas is so tough," she said, and now she was laughing at him, tears filling up her eyes, and he could tell that she wasn't a girl at all, was closer to thirty, had pinched lines at the corner of her right eye, smelled like baby powder and cigarettes and dried sweat. "I'll say you sell cell phones at the Meadows Mall. Am I close?"

Thursdays were always busy for David. The children at Barer Academy—the elementary school on the Temple's campus—visited the main Temple every Thursday for lunch, and it was David's job to come by and smile at the children, say a few words to each, make them feel like God had just strolled in for a bite, and thus ensure that their parents wrote out a big fat check at the end of the month for no other reason than that their children were happy.

In truth, it was David's favorite time of the week. It wasn't that he loved children all that much—he didn't especially, not other people's kids, anyway—but that for the hour he spent going kid to kid, he didn't have to pretend. He just sat down next to them and asked them about their day, their life, how things were *going* and never how things *had been*, which was different from what he dealt with normally. With the people of parenting age, it was always about their childhood, how someone had fucked them up and only God or, if he wasn't available, David could help them deal with the past, like it was some constant growling beast that lived next door that only needed to be fed and watered and everything would be okay. The senior citizens all wanted to bitch about how things were better back then, whenever the fuck that was, and then wanted assurances that they were right, that the world had turned to shit, but that they, of course, weren't to blame.

Today, though, David had a feeling he wouldn't be able to find the focus to deal with the kids, not with what he saw on the embalmer's table down at the Temple mortuary. At three o'clock he was supposed to bury someone named Vincent Castiglione, whose tombstone would read Vincent Castleberg, since Bennie liked to keep things simple. Bennie told David that morning that it was a Chicago guy so they didn't need to worry about putting on too much of a show. "I rounded up a couple old timers to throw dirt," he told David. "So just keep it short and sweet on the last words crap. Believe me, this guy doesn't deserve what we're giving him."

David went down to the Temple's mortuary at 11:30 to check on the stiff, like he always did with the Chicago guys if they came in whole, so that way he wouldn't be surprised if it was someone he grew up with, on the off chance the casket opened. Since it was a Jewish cemetery, it was always closed casket, but in the years David had been attending to the funerals, particularly those embalmed and entombed by employees of Bennie's, he noticed slightly less attention to detail when it concerned enemies of state. Still, when he got down to the mortuary and found Vincent Castiglione belly up on the embalming table still fully dressed in his police uniform, right down to his holster and gun, even though Vincent's head was sitting on the counter inside a plastic bag, the ligature marks on his neck bright purple, it took David a bit by surprise.

"Sorry, Rabbi," the kid working the table said. "Mr. Savone said this is how he asked to be buried and so, we, uh, we, just, uh . . ."

David put a hand up to stop the kid from speaking. He could never remember this dumb fuck's name. He was a

Mexican, some gangbanger Bennie rescued from the pound a few years back and set up in mortuary science classes out in Arizona. Two years later he was wearing a shirt and tie and was cleaning the dead for the Family. A good job, probably. Ruben Something Or Other. He'd done a nice job on Rabbi Kales, David remembered that. "Shut the fuck up," David said, and Ruben's eyes opened wide. David couldn't remember the last time he swore out loud in public, but from the look on Ruben's face, it had the desired effect. "Strip this motherfucker clean, you hear me?"

"Yes, Rabbi," he said.

"You get his clothes, personal effects, all that shit on his belt, including the gun, put it in a bag, something heavy. You got something canvas here?"

"Yes, Rabbi," he said. Ruben reached under a cupboard and came up with a large black canvas bag marked with hazardous waste symbols on either side. "We use these for our uniform cleaning."

David paused, tried to think, looked at Ruben, saw that the kid had a jade pinkie ring, two-carat diamond earrings, a thick platinum bracelet. Fucking thief was probably making six figures and he was still pinching from the dead. "You keep anything?"

"Like his organs?"

"No, you stupid wetback motherfucker," David said, feeling it now, finding the parlance again, how easy it was to hear Sal's voice in his mouth after so many years, though he felt a little sorry for calling the kid a wetback, particularly since he was probably born in Las Vegas. "You steal a clip? Maybe his badge? Something to show the boys later?"

Ruben exhaled deeply, walked back to a small desk in the corner of the embalming room, and pulled open a drawer, rifled around a bit, like he couldn't find what he was looking for, though David knew better so he kept his glare on the kid, and eventually came out with a wallet. "I think Bennie said I could hold onto this," Ruben said, though he handed it to David like it was contagious.

"From now on," David said, because it just felt so good to be on this train again, "you don't think. Got it?"

"Yes, Rabbi," Ruben said.

David watched as Ruben removed all the clothes from the body. Aware that Ruben was probably coming to conclusions of his own today, David tried to remain nonchalant with the process, absently thumbing through the officer's wallet. There was over three grand in folded hundreds in the wallet, along with a handful of gold credit cards. Fucking Chicago cops. When he was younger, David thought of them as the enemy even though half of them were more crooked than he was, but now he understood they were just guys with shitty jobs trying, like he had, to make the grass green. You earned it, partner.

When Ruben was finished stripping the body, he stuffed everything into the bag and then sealed it up with medical tape and set it down in front of David. "That's all of it," Ruben said.

David hefted the bag up and bounced it a little, making sure he could feel the weight of the gun, probably a Glock. Ruben was still standing in front of him, though he didn't look too terribly respectful. He had this sneer on his face that David thought made the kid look like he'd eaten some bad clams, but which probably scared a lot of people not used to seeing how people really looked when they were angry. The one thing about being a thug and a rabbi, David had learned, was that it was nice always feeling vaguely feared and respected at the same time. Now, though, he'd have to do a little bridge building, as Rabbi Kales used to say, if he wanted to make sure things didn't get beyond his control.

"I'm sorry I called you a wetback," David said and handed Ruben the cash from the wallet. Ruben nodded and pocketed the money. "I got a little caught up in the moment." Ruben nodded again. Didn't anyone know how to accept an apology anymore? David took one last look around, figuring that the next time he saw a room like this, he'd be the one on the table, and then realized he'd forgotten something important. "Tell me something, Ruben," David said, back in the voice of Rabbi David Cohen. "What do you intend to do with the head?"

Ruben just shrugged. "I dunno, Rabbi. What are you going to do with the uniform and gun?"

David thought about this, figured the truth would serve him here; figured that was where he was now, toward a path of more obvious truth. "I'm going to take them home, wash both, and then go from there."

As far as exit strategies went, David had to admit that his was a little hastily drawn, but when it's go time, it's go time. It was 3:15, and though he didn't need to do it, he'd gone full bore with his eulogy of the newly minted Vincent Castleberg, which didn't seem to bother the five octogenarians Bennie had assembled for the funeral. He recognized a couple of the men from other funerals, but now couldn't remember if they were for real funerals or fake ones. It didn't really matter, since these guys were so old and so mobbed up that even if he'd pulled out his dick and jerked off onto the casket, they'd keep quiet about it. Bennie always plied the old wise guys with lunch and a couple bucks for their time and then had his boys chauffer them back to their houses at Sun City.

But since David had decided that today was his last fucking day cutting dicks and burying pricks and listening to the world's problems while completely ignoring his own issues—the Hasidic rabbis always talked about this, David realized, saying that if you had proper remorse for your sin, you actually got closer to God, actually became a better person, whereas depression made you a sad, violent, insolent fuck, or, well, something a lot like that—he figured he ought to put things in proper perspective for the late Vincent Castiglione, née Castleberg. So he eulogized himself, instead.

He told the five men about his family life, about his father working as a union millwright, dying young from smoking and drinking (though he'd actually been thrown off of a building), about how he ended up running with some guys from the neighborhood who taught him which joints broke the easiest (this got a knowing nod from the guys), how his mom ended up remarrying and moving to Florida after he graduated from high school, how he fell in love with this sweet girl named Jennifer who made him happy, how he ended up getting into the business and made some poor choices in regards to an important contract and ended up "retiring" to Las Vegas, finding God, and, well, the rest was history. David changed a few important details, naturally, but found that the more he told his story, the better he felt about the choice he was about to make.

David finished with the burial Kaddish, surprised to hear the men each mutter "amen" at the proper times, and then watched as the faux mourners went about tossing clumps of dirt on the coffin. The most ambulatory of the men, dressed smartly in light blue slacks and a white shirt, both originally purchased sometime in the 1970s, walked over and shook David's hand. "A fine service," he said. "Really got the spirit of the poor fucker, if you pardon the expression. I'm not a Jew, but ten, fifteen years from now, if I die, I'd be happy to have you put me in the dirt."

David drove back to his house and packed up what he'd need for his trip—he'd been paid in cash for fifteen years and didn't spend too much of his own money, so he had enough to last him a long time if he was able to last a long time, or, at least, Jennifer and William might have a chance for a decent life; a better life, anyway—and then took his laptop outside to poach his neighbor's wi-fi signal, purchased a one-way ticket back to Chicago using Vincent Castiglione's Visa card, first class, leaving McCarron at 7:00 PM, a little over three hours from now, plenty of time for him to do what he needed to do and then hit the highway. And then David destroyed his laptop, beating it to death with the butt of Castiglione's Glock.

It felt good smashing the computer, but it felt better to have a gun in his hand again. David tried to think of the last time he'd really beaten someone good with a gun, but couldn't draw a bead. Used to be . . . Well, fuck it, David thought, used to be's don't count anymore, just like Neil Diamond said. David worked up a nice sweat pounding on the computer, got himself warm for the task at hand.

Vincent Castiglione was a little thicker through the middle than David, but his uniform fit well enough. If he had more time, David would run it through the washer and dryer again, see if he could get the uniform to shrink, get some more of that dead stink out of it, too. Still, he did stop to look at himself in the mirror before leaving the house, and it was like getting a glimpse at an alternate life: Sal Cupertine looked pretty good as a cop, David decided. He checked his watch. It was nearly five o'clock. He thought about what Bennie would look like when he saw David in a cop's uniform; what Bennie would look like with a hole in the middle of his fat fucking face courtesy of Vincent Castiglione's service Glock. He thought about how, once he was on the road, cops would search airports in Las Vegas and Chicago for Castiglione; how they would swarm the home of Bennie Savone, once Bennie's wife found him without his face. David was sure they'd recognize the uniform on Bennie's video surveillance. He took one last look around his own home. Sal Cupertine could have been Sgt. Cupertine. A real fucking mensch.

# Walls

**W**e were not consulted. It was the 1970s. And then it was the early 1980s. What would happen was that men would come to the door, smelling of Brute, or smelling of cigarettes and the fine leather interior of their Gran Torinos or TR7s, and they would say, "I'm here to pick up Sally. This the right house?"

We'd say, "Yeah, come on in. She's getting dressed." Or we'd say, "Do you mean Mommy?" Or, and this was rare, but it happened because we were young and angry and when your parents have divorced and all you have to show for it is a mother who has suddenly decided that she'd like to fuck as many men as possible, and a father who it turns out was gay but you wouldn't know that until long after he was dead and you found the photos and the letters, but who, at the time, was dating a woman named Miss Lisa who hosted *Romper Room* on Channel 2, we'd say, "Are you our new daddy?" It was cruel, but we were smart and we were sad and we had agendas.

We kept a list. We updated it nightly. We remember you. That's what this is all about. We remember you. We thought you'd stay. We thought, on the day before the last night, when you sat us down and said that you'd stay but that our mother was crazy, was ruining your life, was ruining our lives, too, and if you had any legal rights, why, you'd take us out of this house. You told us you'd just wait until our mother went to work and you'd back up a big truck and we'd all just move our stuff into it. We'd take the two dogs, Sam and Roxanne, and we'd pull up the yellow shag carpet in the family room, the hundreds of *Star Wars* action figures, the posters of Peter Frampton, the posters of Rick Springfield, the posters of Heather Thomas, the Easy-Bake Oven, the RISK board, the photo albums from when we still had the beach house, back when Mom still looked so young, still had that Jackie O thing going for her. Dad used to be in those photos, too, but he's gone, cut out, just a shoulder or a foot or the brim of a hat barely visible in a jagged corner.

You were a cop, we remember that. But then you quit your job after you saw a guy get his head blown off. BLAM, you said. BLAM. And then there was nothing but a stump. You said that's what made you quit your job and become a steel worker, and then you lost that job because people had a way of dying around you. People had a way of being near you and then not being near you. They said you didn't follow protocol. That you were responsible for an industrial accident. And so you lived in our house for a little while, and that was good. We felt so calm. We felt normal. We felt the wall shake when you had sex with our mother, but that was okay. And we felt the wall shake when you'd climb into her shower and sob, banging your fists against the tile, probably unaware that her bathroom backed up to one of our bedrooms.

We remember you.

We remember Doug Loomis. He called accidentally, looking for someone else, but Mom liked his voice, told him she thought he sounded very interesting, wondered if he might like to buy her a drink the next time he was in town. She called him "Wrong Number," and she told us he had a boat and that he really wanted to take us all out on it; that we'd sail to Catalina, or Hawaii, or Peru, and that he loved all of us kids. Doug Loomis was bald. Doug Loomis showed up in our kitchen one Sunday morning and asked us to make him some coffee. Asked us to get him the newspaper. Asked us if we could quiet the fuck down. Mom wanted to know, a few days later, what we'd done to "Wrong Number," because he no longer called, not even by accident.

You once took us to a park and told us to forget who our parents were. You told us to pretend that you were our father and that the woman who'd just thrown a platter of frozen meat at us was a burglar.

We remember Cy Cohen. Cy Cohen sold Seiko watches. In the morning, he'd walk outside in one of our father's old bathrobes and he'd read the paper standing up on the driveway. Cy Cohen drove an Alfa Romeo. Cy Cohen used to scream his own name at night. It sounded like this: "Oh, fuck yes, Cy!" Cy Cohen lasted a few weeks, actually, long enough to enjoy Thanksgiving in our home. He gave us all Seiko watches. He left them on doilies next to our plates. They were thick and silver. They glowed in the dark. They pulled our wrists down. They kept imperfect time. Mom told us Cy cared very deeply for us, would probably want to adopt us, that he loved us very much. We wrote excessively long thank-you notes to Cy for the watches. A week after Cy Cohen stopped his eponymous joy, he showed up at the house and demanded all of our watches back.

You told us we'd be eighteen one day. You told us to hold onto that.

We remember Mark Barton. Mark had three kids, all boys, and they were big scary fucks. They went to school with us. They used to beat the shit out of us. They once tied us to the bike racks in front of Castle Rock Elementary and threw walnuts at our genitals. They said things like, "We're going to make your pussies bleed." Mark Barton owned a chain of hardware stores. He wore golf shirts with a penguin logo. He had silver hair that he kept cut short, like he was in the military. Mark Barton starred in his own commercials where he'd say, "Hi, Kids! I'm Mark Barton. Go get your parents and tell them I'm on TV and want to make a deal with them!" Mom met Mark Barton when she was thinking about becoming a realtor. She went to some community mixer where he was the toastmaster. She didn't come home for two days, just left a message on the Record-A-Call that said she'd met someone, that we should eat the Swanson Chicken TV Dinners in the freezer, that we should ask Stephanie Howser's mom to drive us to school. The three Barton boys cornered us at school and told us that our mother sounded like a malfunctioning backhoe when she was getting fucked, that she made shitty pancakes, and that if we weren't careful, they'd make our pussies bleed.

Your sister died while you were living in our house. We went to the funeral even though we didn't know her. It was December, a few days before Christmas, and the service was held out in Benicia. In the distance, we could see the Navy Mothball Fleet docked out in the shallow bay. You got up during the service and said that you were sorry that you'd been such a terrible brother to her; that you'd let her make so many mistakes; that you should have just picked her up in your arms and carried her away, put her in a place where she could get the help she needed, where she wouldn't find a way to meet guys like you, Freddie, you fucking cocksucker. You made eye contact with us. We nodded our heads and mouthed that we loved you. We went to Farrell's afterward and ate hot fudge sundaes. You told us stories about your sister. You told us she lived in regret. You told us her negativity propelled her toward drugs and guys like Freddie who would rather kick her fucking ass than kiss her on the lips. When Mom said not to use such language in front of us, you said, "You remind me of her a lot, Sally. You really do. That's not a compliment."

We remember Jack Merken. Jack wore velour. Jack went to Purdue on a basketball scholarship in some nebulous, yellowed past, but that didn't stop him from wearing Purdue sweatshirts and Purdue T-shirts and velour pullover V-neck sweaters with a tiny Purdue logo stitched over the chest. Jack Merken owned a limo service and said he had a house up in Tahoe. Every time he came to pick up Mom, a long, black limo would pull up in front of our house. "Jack's here," we'd say, watching him through the living room window, his shadow barely visible as he slid through the opening between the front seat and the back seat so he could get out through the back passenger door. The neighbors would come out onto their front porches to see who was in the limo, because this was in the 1970s and not just anyone could get a limo, unless you had $75 to spend for the evening. We got to drive in the limo once. It was raining, and we pounded on the master bedroom door to let Mom know we needed a ride to school, that all of us would be drenched if we walked, that there was lightning that might kill us. Jack came to the door. "Your mom says to ask the neighbors for a ride," Jack said, "but why don't I take you?" We climbed into the back of the limo and it was nothing like we imagined. The seats were once crushed red velvet, but now they were crusted and hard, black electrical tape keeping them together in places. It smelled of perfume and cigars and something like vinegar, but more pungent. We found a bra on the floor. We found a high-heeled shoe. We found Marlboro butts in the ashtray. We found handprints on the back window. We found Jack staring at us through the dividing window at the stop sign on the corner of our street. It looked like he wanted to cry, or he wanted to cough, or he wanted this moment in his life to end, because he just kept staring at us before finally saying, "I'm sorry. You guys should just walk."

You took us for lobster on the day your unemployment ran out.

We remember Dan Kern. Dan was our stepfather for six months. Dan was a lawyer. Dan spoke German fluently. Dan wore bikini underwear long before it was fashionable. Dan had three children from a previous marriage, though all of them were adopted. Steven, Bonnie, and Lyle came to live with us on weekends, sharing our rooms, eating our Pop-Tarts, changing the TV from reruns of *The Brady Bunch* to reruns of *Get Smart* without even asking. Dan didn't particularly care for the fact that we didn't call him Dad. He asked us if we loved him. We said no. He asked us why not. We told him we didn't even know him. Mom told us he was going to adopt us, and we were going to change our last names, and that Dan was going to get full custody of his kids and we'd all live together in a big house in Pacific Heights. Then Steven beat up his grandma with a broomstick and told everyone that Johnny Carson told him to do it. Then Bonnie brought a Ouija board to our house and started taking her top off around us, which caused problems, because we weren't related and we were young and we knew from the shaking wall that there was possibility in all of this, that we could all scream our names and no one would know what it meant but us. Then Lyle showed up at homecoming dressed as a woman, and we found out that he had the machinery to be both and he'd made a choice, because he was sixteen, and he was now Linda. One day shortly thereafter, Dan chased us all into the garage. He was wearing his Hawaiian print bikini underwear and was waving around a butcher knife and screamed at us in German. And then he wasn't our stepfather anymore.

You showed up at our graduations. We saw you in the back. It had been years, but we recognized you. We looked for you afterward, and since we never found you, we began to think that maybe you weren't really there, were just a mirage, just us wishing you'd reappear.

We remember when there was no one left. We remember when the men stopped coming because Mom had become sick, was told she'd be dead in six months, though of course she never did die. But by then we were gone. We came back as adults to care for her, back to our old bedrooms. We slept on our *Star Wars* sheets. We listened to The Knack and Gordon Lightfoot and Journey and REO Speedwagon and The Thompson Twins and Shaun Cassidy and Blondie and talked about how much those songs used to mean to us, so much so that when Mom would scream "Down or off!" we'd just turn it up and wait for the rage, wait for her to walk outside and turn off the power, leaving us in the dark, spinning the records on our old Fisher-Price record players, the music just tinny scratches of sound, a departure from the yelling that rippled down the hallway, that caused Sam and Roxanne, the dogs, to crap themselves right where they stood. We found Bonnie's Ouija board and tried to contact you there, in case you were dead. We stood Mom up in her shower and bathed her, the water glancing off the tile wall and pooling at our feet, and we imagined you standing there alone, hitting that wall, pounding that wall, sobbing, and we reached out to you in our minds in case you stood there still, haunting the shower, your demons buried in the grout along with bits of skin from your knuckles. We put Mom into her bed, and it seemed so much smaller than we imagined it. Just a bed. Four corners. Sheets. A headboard. We imagined you there beside her. We tried to figure out what drove you there in the first place. How old were you? Thirty-five? Forty? Our age now. We have our own beds. We have our own master bedrooms, and yet we think of you still, standing here, saying good-bye to her in bed, because that's where it happened. You stood in the doorway of the master bedroom, and you said, "I just can't do this. How many others, Sally? How many?" And she said a number like five or seven or who fucking cares just get the fuck out you no-job son of a bitch. And you walked down the hallway and poked your head into each of our rooms and you said good-bye and you said sorry and you said you tried for us but that there's a limit and you'd found yours, and then the stapler hit you in the back and we looked and Mom was throwing things from her bedroom at you. You just kept walking. You even stopped and hugged the dogs. You put your nose in that space between Sam's eyes and you held her ears and you whispered something. And you picked up Roxanne, who was a collie, and you hugged her like a child and she licked your face. A bottle of your cologne came sailing down through the air and it cracked on the wall and you didn't even move. The hallway still smells of you. Mom would have us shampoo the carpet and scrub the wallpaper, but nothing removed the smell. Here we are, decades in the dust, and we find tiny bits of glass still wedged into the wall.

You exist on the Internet. We've MapQuested your addresses. One day we will fly to you in Florida and Iowa and Alaska and Washington and we will knock on your door and when you open it we will say, "Do you remember us?" And you will say no and you will say no and you will say no and then maybe you will say yes. Because it will be you and not just a man with your name. You'll be older, too, because there isn't a way for memory to freeze the body like it freezes trauma in place.

Or we will let you be, give you that grace. We will drive by your homes across the country and we will imagine you inside and we will wonder if you've known all along that we remember.

# Palm Springs

**U**sed to be Tania hated taking the bus anywhere. She didn't want to become one of those people who brought the bus up in every conversation, as if it were part of her life and not just how she got from one place to another. Like her friend Jean, back when she was still living in Reno and working at the Cal-Neva. They'd sit in the smokeroom during breaks—back when they still had a smokeroom—and Jean would always have some story to tell about the bus. There was the time a guy had a heart attack in his seat and died before the bus could even come to a complete stop. There was the time a little girl fell off her seat and bit through her bottom lip and ended up bleeding on Jean's new shoes. There was even the time Jean swore she saw Bill Cosby on the bus and that he was just as sweet as could be and had asked for her phone number.

Tania wonders now, as she steps aboard the #14 that will take her from her apartment in Desert Hot Springs to the Chuyalla Indian Casino in downtown Palm Springs, whatever became of Jean. After Tania left Reno for Las Vegas in 1985, they exchanged letters for a few months, though Tania quickly realized she didn't have much to write about other than the weather or various personal calamities: a broken toe that kept her from cocktailing for a week, a winter heat wave that blew out her car's AC, her cocker, Lucy, getting into an ant hill. And so she just stopped writing or responding to Jean, eventually tossing out Jean's letters unopened. Tania remembers a vague sense of guilt concerning this whole episode, but in retrospect it all seems petty. Just because you're friends with someone doesn't mean you have to stay friends with them. Sometimes it's just easier to be without.

And anyway, what would they have to talk about today if they were still friends? Yes, better all around.

Settling into her regular seat—third from the left—Tania can't help but think Jean would find Tania's present condition all very ironic, particularly since back then Tania used to tease her constantly about "taking the limo" to work every day, even when Tania offered to pick her up in her Honda when they worked the same shift. She loved that car: a black Honda Accord with leather seats, a cassette player with a detachable face, six speakers. She remembers how important it was that she have six speakers, how she obsessed over the sound quality in her car, how she rolled down the windows on even the hottest days so that passing strangers could hear her stereo. Twenty-three years old then and the thing she was most proud of was a set of goddamned speakers.

Tania closes her eyes when the bus leaves the curb. The ride from Desert Hot Springs to the casino takes between thirty-seven and forty-eight minutes, depending upon whether or not the bus stops at all of the benches along the way. It's a Sunday morning, so she figures she's only got thirty-seven today, seeing as the bus is stone empty. She likes to close her eyes for the trip, though she never sleeps, because she knows it's the only time for the next nine hours she'll get the chance to see darkness. Cocktailing in a casino isn't like what it used to be. Back in Reno, they kept it midnight inside the casino: black ceiling, purple carpet, blood red walls. These days it's all bright lights and warm yellows everywhere. The young girls think it's soothing, but Tania finds it irritating, wonders why anyone would want to see so much. What she wouldn't give to have missed a few things. Forty-seven years old now, Tania figures she could unsee ten, fifteen years and be happy about it.

Sometimes, when she's done looking for her adopted daughter, Natalya, on the Internet, or chatting about her with other mothers online, Tania tries to find her twenty-three-year-old self on the Ouija board she bought at Toys "R" Us. She figures if a Ouija board can supposedly talk to the dead or people living in other dimensions, it might very well have the ability to reach back in time, too. It hasn't worked yet, but Tania thinks that maybe she's just not asking the right questions, thinks that maybe all she needs to do is find someone else to do the Ouija with her, double up on the spirit power, you see, and maybe that'll do it. And when she finds herself, she'll tell her to sell that fucking car and concentrate on getting her shit right, because the future is painted in bright colors, baby, and no one will notice you.

In all her years working at casinos in Reno, Las Vegas, and now Palm Springs, Tania has only hit it big once. It was 1996, back when everyone had money, and she was working at the Mirage in Las Vegas. After a particularly good night—Tania can't remember what that means anymore, but when she tells everyone about Las Vegas in the 90s, she tells them she pocketed between two and three grand on a weekend night, though that sounds absurd now, the truth probably a good 50 percent below the mythology—she put $500 down on a hand of Caribbean Stud and flopped a royal, and just like that she was $50,000 richer. Taxes took fifteen off the top, leaving Tania with thirty-five; still more than enough at the time to put a down payment on a nice house in Las Vegas, something with a great room, a nice yard, room for a pool, maybe even something on a golf course if she really kept banking at her job. Plus, she still had good credit back then, unlike most of her friends who had to keep changing their phone numbers to stay a few months ahead of the collection agencies, and she loved living in Las Vegas.

Five hours into her shift at the Chuyalla Indian Casino and with just $37 in tips, Tania can't imagine ever risking $500 on paper again; because, really, she thinks now, making her tenth round this hour through the blackjack tables, that's all gambling is: placing hope in colored paper. She wonders sometimes if her life wouldn't have been better if, instead of betting $500 on cards, she'd taken that money to a stationery store and purchased reams of 25-weight linen resume paper. Maybe that investment would have forced her into a better life, one where success was predicated on having something to put on all that paper.

Tania drops off three White Russians, five beers, and a Tom Collins to a kid who is clearly underage, since no one under seventy would have the audacity to order a Tom Collins, and no one over twenty-one would even consider uttering it around a pack of their friends. Not when they could order Courvoisier and pretend to be 2Pac. Do kids still listen to

2Pac? She supposes they do, but Tania remembers listening to him when he was alive, before he became some martyr, and thinking he was just okay, just another guy with mommy issues, like half the men she'd hooked up with since high school. When she decided to adopt Natalya, she threw out her entire gangsta rap CD collection, figuring it wouldn't be appropriate for her new role as a mother to be singing along to songs about hustling. Plus, she wanted to like what Natalya liked.

Tania winds back to the bar and hands the bartender, Gordon, her orders: four beers, a Sex on the Beach, two Johnnie Walkers, three more White Russians. A blackjack table full of marines in from the base at 29 Palms erupts in a flood of loud obscenities just then, prompting half of the casino to turn and stare.

"Classy people out there today," Gordon says. "Barely noon and people are trashed."

"I hate Sundays," Tania says. "People should just go home. Watch TV. Read the Bible. Something."

"It's algebra," Gordon says. "In order for other people to have a good time, we have to suffer their stupidity, and then someone else will have to hose their puke off the parking lot. All together, we get off pretty good."

"I'll be lucky to walk with fifty," Tania says. "You know what fifty gets you? Nothing. It's not even worth it to come in for fifty. Once I pay for the bus, get lunch, pick up dinner on the way home, what have I got left? It's not worth it."

Gordon places the four beers on her tray, and for a moment Tania considers picking up one of them and just downing it, maybe lining up a couple shots, too, see how the day passes with a little less clarity on things. Back in Las

Vegas you could rail a line and . . . well . . . No, Tania thinks, you just can't compare your life along some arbitrary timeline, can't think of yourself as a compare and contrast. The past was different. The present is ever changing. No, it has to be about what comes next. About staying focused. Keep yourself together. Gather resources. Find Natalya. Don't force an apology. Fix things. Get a family. Buy Christmas presents. Move to the city, any city, but get out of casinos and hotels and bars. Maybe.

"How long you lived in the desert?" Tania asks. Gordon is new—she's seen him a couple of times in the last month, but this is the first shift he's been on alone—so they haven't found that rhythm yet, only know each other enough to flirt a little, tell a joke or two. Nothing personal. But for some reason today Tania feels like talking and can't stand to listen to the other cocktail girls on the floor. They call her "Mom" and always want her to listen to their problems, Sundays inevitably taken up by whatever horror happened at the club the night previous, or whatever drama they have with their "baby daddies," a term Tania just can't wrap her mind around. When did people stop being parents? But Gordon seems nice, maybe even smart. Smarter than her other choices, anyway.

"Five years, plus or minus," Gordon says. "I used to come here when I was a kid, you know? I remember my dad once drove us right up to Bob Hope's front gate and we got chased off by dogs. Big old Dobermans. I'll never forget that."

"I can't see myself being here that long," Tania says. Gordon puts the rest of Tania's drinks down and then rechecks the order. No one ever does that, Tania thinks; no one else here gives a damn if they screw up my money.

"Oh," Gordon says, "you live here a while it becomes like anywhere else. You find your shit, you know? This town, I can bartend until I'm sixty-five, seventy, and no one would think differently about me. Maybe along the way I find a rich old woman who wants to take care of a hot young stud like me, I hold her hand for a few years, take her to her Botox appointments, and then, one day, she dies in her sleep and I'm a millionaire." Gordon's laughing now, but Tania sees something sad in his face, like he's not just joking around, like part of him believes this might be his best chance for a good life.

"You've got it figured out," Tania says.

"Presuming I don't blow my head off first," he says.

"You don't seem the suicide type," Tania says.

"They'd just prop me behind the bar. It wouldn't be much difference. But if you stick around until I get my millions," Gordon says, "I'll let you move into my guest house. We'll sit around the saltwater pool all day reading thrillers and sipping cognac."

"I see myself moving somewhere with a bit more character. A little history. Less tourists. All my life, I've been stuck with tourists."

"Like Maine or somewhere?"

"Somewhere," Tania says.

"No way for me," Gordon says. "I'm California bred and spread." Another girl—Tania can never remember if her name is Cindy or Bonnie, so she just calls her "sweetie"— slams her order on the counter, prompting Gordon to glare at her. "To be continued," he says. "Don't pack your bags for Maine just yet."

Really Tania was thinking about Russia—Tula, Russia, specifically—but telling Gordon that would mean she'd have to explain her situation, and she just isn't emotionally prepared for that, at least not at work. Talking about Natalya here would make her trivial.

Even still, going back to Russia has been on her mind constantly these days. Maybe Natalya went back. Maybe there was an email from Natalya waiting for Tania right this instant telling her to come back to Tula, that she was sorry, too, and that she'd love to see her mother.

Before she picked up Natalya in Tula, Tania imagined Russia would be a perpetually gray country filled with scary Communists, like the ones they used to show marching in Red Square, back when Ronald Reagan used to scare her, too. Everyone told her to be careful, tell people she was Canadian so they wouldn't kill her, to be as inconspicuous as possible.

But when she finally arrived—she remembered the date exactly: February 22, 1997—after flying into Moscow and then driving for two hours with an administrator from the orphanage, she couldn't get over how beautiful the country was, how pleasant the people she met seemed to be, how *substantial* everything felt. The administrator kept pointing out interesting landmarks between Moscow and Tula, talked about Peter the Great, discussed the rich mining history of the city. And what a city: Citadels from the sixteenth century. Lush green forests surrounding the Upa River. Museums honoring famous writers and warriors. It was nothing like Las Vegas, nothing like Reno, nothing like any place she'd ever visited. She wondered even then what it might be like to settle in Russia, to raise her child in her home country, to live in such a place! Yes, she'd come back here when Natalya was fully integrated as an American. Adopting a twelve-year-old would present problems, she knew that, but Tania thought that later in life they would travel back here together, maybe buy a little house. Tania was thirty-five then, just twenty-three years older than her new daughter. Young enough that they'd be like friends the older Natalya got, less like mother and daughter.

So foolish, Tania thinks, grabbing up her tray. All of it.

Adopting Natalya wasn't something Tania planned. It was the money that did it. Well, the money and loneliness. A few weeks after she hit the royal, Tania's fifteen-year-old dog, Lucy, woke up one morning and urinated blood; three hours later Tania watched while her vet quietly inserted a needle into her dog's right front paw to put her to sleep (a term Tania has never liked, as the implication is that the dog will someday wake up and be just fine), and just like that, after fifteen years and three hours, she was completely alone.

Oh, she still had family and friends then; people she honestly loved at some point. But when it all boiled away, the fact was that she just didn't keep people very well. Her parents and older sister, Justine, still sent her Christmas and birthday gifts, invited her to their homes for Thanksgiving (they even offered money if she couldn't afford a plane ticket from Las Vegas, since her parents lived in Spokane and her sister in San Francisco), called once a week—and she enjoyed talking to them, but afterward couldn't recount a single aspect of the conversation.

She'd had a series of boyfriends, too. Most of them long-term affairs, actually, and at the time had just broken up with a DJ at the Rio after he accepted a six-month gig on a cruise ship, but their relationship hadn't even been intimate. All things being equal, sitting on the sofa at home and talking to her dog was preferable most of the time anyway.

That night, though, her dog dead, her parents and sister filled with the kind of comfort people without pets usually provide—"What you should do tomorrow is go to a rescue and pick up an abused dog," her father said—she sat alone on her sofa and watched a documentary on HBO about the plight of children in Russian orphanages. By the film's conclusion, Tania decided to make something of her life, to put her royal winnings to good use, give someone a chance at a better life, allow that money to be more than just a house she'd struggle to pay for night after night. She'd found the perfect place in Summerlin—a three bedroom with a little lap pool out back, Corian counters throughout, a view of the Red Rock Mountains—and was preparing to make an offer, though she didn't even know what that meant. Either she'd buy or she wouldn't, and she hadn't.

No, she didn't need a house. Tania knew her life was disposable, as if someone could cut her head off and paste it on another girl's body, and the world wouldn't notice at all. She needed to *become*. She would adopt a child from Russia. She would look into dental hygienist school—several girls she'd worked with at the Mirage were studying at the community college during the day to become hygienists, and it sounded like a good job, albeit one spent on your feet all day bent over people, which in concept sounded not much different than cocktailing.

She'd always had maternal instincts. Tania had even been pregnant once, if only for a few weeks. Her boyfriend Clive got her pregnant—this was when she was thirty—and

Tania spent an entire long weekend off from work shopping for baby clothes at Target, rummaging through garage sales for baby carriages and strollers and figuring out how to decorate the baby's room. It was too soon, she knew that, as she'd only just missed her period, but she'd taken an at-home test and had an appointment to see her gynecologist for the following week and felt a great desire to begin this new phase of her life, sure that being a mother wasn't so much a calling for her now as it was a station: a chance to be a better person. She was certain she'd need to move in order to get away from Clive, who, while he was a fun guy to waste time with, would be a terrible father. It wasn't that he'd ever hit her or even been particularly cruel, only that he was stupid, and stupid would not do as a role model. No, she decided, she'd just move up to Spokane with her child—who she thought she'd name Corey no matter the sex—and her own father could play that positive role until she found someone smart, someone who didn't work at a restaurant or bar. When she miscarried a few days later, she broke up with Clive to pay penance for her own conceit; to bring a child into this world, when they couldn't even save the dolphins or blue whales or whatever, well, it was just silly. A dog would do. Yes. A dog would be enough until things felt more stable all around. But even now, in the small storage locker she has in her building in Desert Hot Springs, there's a box marked "Corey" that she's hauled around across two states and several years.

When she woke up the morning after seeing the documentary and couldn't get the idea of adopting a Russian child out of her mind, couldn't stop thinking that her life had been lived in service, strictly service, and that this was her chance to actually be a real human, to get off her ass and make something stable for someone else, she knew she had to act. She had to learn to keep something, to not spontaneously rid herself of responsibility.

What Tania didn't realize was how long and arduous and pricey the whole experience would be. It took just over a year between the day her dog died and the exact moment she stepped off the airplane in Las Vegas with her daughter (*her daughter!*) by her side. She spent eleven months searching for the right child, filling out the paperwork, getting the approvals, paying the fees—it was $20,000 to the Russian agencies, another $5,000 for lawyers and paperwork stateside—until, in the end, she had to ask her parents if she could borrow another $5,000 just to get to Russia, where she'd need to stay for a month to attend adoption hearings and to get Natalya legal for her arrival in the U.S. Her parents ended up giving her $10,000, told her it wasn't a loan, that it was a gift, that they were so proud of her.

Natalya lived with Tania for five years. Five good years, Tania thinks now, dropping off drinks in the slot aisles for nickel and quarter tips, though like everything else about the past, she's sure that's just the romantic version. She loved Natalya, though. This Tania is sure of. And if Natalya never really loved her, that's okay, too. She'd given Natalya the chance and there was worth in that.

After her shift ends at six, Tania walks down Palm Canyon Drive and looks into the shop windows, examining the silly T-shirts and bumper stickers ("What happens in Palm Springs, stays in Palm Springs . . . usually in a Time Share"), the gaudy jewelry only a vacationer would find the impulse for, the fancy clothes she never sees inside the casino, but assumes someone must wear somewhere. She's always reading about these gala charities and benefit balls held in Palm Springs but can't imagine who the people are who attend such things or where they buy their clothes. Surely none of them pile into the Mercedes and come to the tourist traps to do their shopping.

Tania pauses in front of Chico's and peers inside at the shoppers, all of whom look to be around her age, but are infected with what she thinks of as Realtoritis: their hair about five years past the trend, their tans rubbed on, their heels inappropriately high. And yet they exude an air of success, as if by showing property they somehow glean personal value.

She wonders, if she were a dental hygienist—if she somehow managed to finally pass chemistry, which she failed three times while she lived in Las Vegas, twice in the year she waited on the adoption, once in the six months after Natalya ran away (and really, she didn't run away, she just left)—if people would be able to tell just by looking at her. Maybe she might be mistaken for a doctor occasionally. That wouldn't be so awful. And maybe people would treat her with respect without understanding why they did it. Cocktailing was never her dream job, but then nothing else struck her as all that compelling, either. When she was young, if there was a chance to fuck up, Tania usually took it, just to see what it felt like. And the result was that she felt, after forty-seven years, that she'd lived, even if she didn't really have much to show for it anymore.

The idea of being a hygienist was a good one, and she really pursued it during that year of waiting, if nothing else because it looked good on all of her applications. She wasn't just a cocktail waitress, she was "studying to become a dental hygienist," and people at the various agencies seemed to treat that with some dignity. But now, staring at the women trying on skirts too short by a decade, she thinks that it's all the same in the end. Just a job. Just a way to afford the things you want. Tania doesn't *want* anything anymore. She *needs* to find Natalya, if only to know that she's alive, but even that has quelled some in the intervening years as she's learned how frequently teenagers adopted out of Russia simply pick up and leave when they have a little money or the keys to the car or the PIN code to their parents' ATM card.

Tania checks her watch. She agreed to meet Gordon at 6:30 in front of the statue of former Palm Springs Mayor Sonny Bono that graces a courtyard up the street from the casino. He asked if he could buy her a drink after work, and when she told him she didn't drink anymore, which wasn't strictly true, he didn't flinch. "Then let me buy you a lamp. You must like lights, right? I know a great little lamp store. They even give you the shades and bulbs, too. It's a real deal."

"You're crazy," she said, but agreed to meet him anyway and now was going to be late if she didn't hustle. Sundays were always sad nights for Tania, and the truth was that she was likely to pop some Two Buck Chuck tonight in front of the TV herself, Sundays her night off of the Internet, a night away from her search. Really, it was more a habit now than anything: Check the message board at LostAndFoundChildren.com to see if anyone responded to her photo of Natalya; read the listserv messages from her Yahoo group; scour every search engine, newspaper archive, and blog index on the planet for any mention of Natalya's known names. This searching was her infinity. A bottomless hope. But she gave Sundays up after her own mother told her to start weaning herself, that she had to grasp the idea that Natalya wasn't really her child, that she'd just been a child who lived with her for a time. "Think of it like a car lease," her mother said. "That's how we've approached it emotionally; she wasn't our granddaughter, just a child who lived with our daughter."

*Like a car lease.* Tania knew her mother meant well and so she tried, on Sundays, to treat Natalya's disappearance like an episode of a TV show that she found particularly emotionally affecting, if only for twenty-four hours.

Up ahead, Tania sees Gordon leaning up against the Sonny Bono statue. He doesn't see her yet, so she takes a few seconds to stare at him, notices that a few of the passing tourist ladies are doing the same. It's late spring and the air smells like a mixture of coconut tanning oil and jacaranda blooms, and it only makes sense that Gordon has changed from his casino uniform into tan pants and a white linen button-down, but for some reason Tania is surprised by this, by how effortlessly casual he looks, how he seems to fit in so perfectly. Even from several yards away Tania can see his tan skin through his shirt, the contours of his body. She wonders how old he is, thinks he's probably thirty-five, maybe thirty-eight, too young for her now, anyway. And what does she know about him? What does she know about anybody anymore?

"There you are," he says when Tania finally approaches him. He puts an arm over her shoulder in a friendly way and gives her a pat, like they're brother and sister. "I thought you were going to ditch me here with Sonny."

"You know I'm forty-seven," she says.

"How would I know that?"

"I'm just telling you," she says.

"Is today your birthday?"

"No," she says.

"Then why are we talking about it?"

"I'm not sure why you asked me out," Tania says. "What we're doing here. That's all."

Gordon exhales, and Tania realizes he's been holding his breath, that he actually seems a little nervous now that she's paying attention. "Can't people go out for a drink, Tania? Isn't that what normal people do?"

"Are we normal people? All day spent watching people fuck up their lives. Who would call that normal?" Gordon nods, but it's clear he's not agreeing to anything, just happy to let Tania vent whatever it is she feels the need to vent. She likes that, though is certain he's just trying to humor her. Give him a break, Tania thinks. Act like a person for an hour, see how it feels. "Where was this lamp store you were talking about? I'm in great need of track lighting."

What Tania remembers about Natalya is insignificant if looked at obliquely. She's realized this before tonight, before she saw Gordon's expression glaze over while she prattled on about the way Natalya used to sneeze every time she ate chocolate, or how Natalya's eyes were brown on some days and green on others, or how, when she's feeling particularly sentimental, she'll spray a bit of Natalya's perfume on her old pillow and will set it down across the room while she's watching television or cooking something, so that she'll just get a whiff of it in the course of doing regular things, and it will be like Natalya's in the other room, sitting on the floor like she used to do with her headphones on, listening to her English language tapes.

She could blame on the liquor this sudden descent into reverie, but that would be useless. As soon as Gordon asked her, "How did you end up in Palm Springs?" she felt it all bubble out, the whole story, from her cocker Lucy dying, to waking up one morning in her townhouse in Las Vegas to find Natalya gone, along with the Ford Explorer, the keys to the safe-deposit box (where Tania—like every other cocktail waitress, bartender, and stripper in Las Vegas—deposited the majority of her tips so she wouldn't have to report them to the IRS), and, most disheartening, three full photo albums of pictures taken since Natalya's arrival.

How did she end up in Palm Springs? She asked herself this question repeatedly, and the answer was always the same: it wasn't Las Vegas. Usually that sufficed, but tonight, sitting across from Gordon, his face getting younger with every passing moment, until she's certain he's no more than thirty-two (unless what's happened is that with each drink and sad detail she's tacked on another month to her own life, so that she's now pushing seventy years old), she knows that she ended up in Palm Springs because it was the only place she could run to where she had no memories, no connections, nothing corporeal to remind her of everything lost, but where the world itself was essentially the same. She could do her job. She could breathe the desert air. She could listen to the dinging of the slots, the whooping of the drunks, the crunching of ice in the blender constantly making margaritas, the drone of mindless cocktail conversation and pretend that her life had frozen in place, that she'd conjured the whole sad affair. Yes, she could close her eyes inside the Chuyalla Indian Casino and imagine herself thirty, childless and disproportionate to reality.

"I've ruined the night," Tania says now. She and Gordon have been sitting at the patio bar in front of the Hyatt for three hours now. There's a man playing acoustic guitar on a small stage a few feet away from them, and every fifteen minutes or so he plays "Margaritaville" and another ten tourists stop to sing along. "I didn't mean to go on like that."

"No, it's fine," Gordon says. He reaches across the table and tries to take her hands in his, but she pulls them back and puts them in her lap before she remembers her own admonition: be human.

"I should go home," she says, forgetting that she doesn't have a car anymore, that she'll need to call a cab or ask Gordon for a ride, since the buses stopped running hours ago. "I'll end up telling you about every boyfriend I've ever had otherwise."

Gordon doesn't smile like she thinks he will. He just stares at her. "Let me ask you something," he says eventually. "You think you'll ever find her?"

"No," Tania says, and for the first time she actually believes it. The truth is that no one has ever asked her this question, though of course it has existed in the subtext of her life all the while; a nagging sense that her search for Natalya was what she *should* be doing, but the fact remained that if Natalya wanted to be found, if Natalya wanted Tania to find her, specifically, it would have already happened. "I may locate her at some point. But I don't think I'll ever see her again."

Tania stares out her sliding glass door as Gordon's taillights disappear down the hill, back toward Palm Springs. It's midnight, and though the air has chilled, Tania feels feverish. She told Gordon, as he pulled up to her complex, that she'd invite him in but that she was afraid she caught a bug sitting outside for so long this evening. She shakes her head thinking about it now, how silly she must have sounded, how ignorant, as if she could catch consumption from sitting outside listening to Jimmy Buffett songs on a spring night.

"It's okay," he said, and Tania sensed relief from Gordon, though the truth is that she's forgotten how to read young men anymore. They used to be so obvious to her, so obscenely obvious, but now they're just mannerisms in her peripheral "There will be other nights. I know where you work."

She kissed him lightly on the cheek and got out of his car, didn't bother to turn and smile or even give a little wave when she got to the top step of the metal staircase that leads to her apartment, though she knew Gordon was watching her. He'd been raised well enough to wait until a woman was inside her home before driving off, but not well enough to be doing something better with his life than bartending at an Indian casino, and that alone made Tania sad for him.

Tania opens the sliding door and steps outside onto her tiny patio. She's arranged three pots of daisies around a single white plastic chair, and though it doesn't seem like much, it's all she can do to just keep those daisies alive and the chair clean enough to sit on. Tonight, though, she stands against the wrought iron railing surrounding the patio and stares south toward the wind farms of Palm Springs, watches as light jumps between the spinning windmill turbines, listens for the low whine of the coyotes that often rummage in the dumpsters behind her building and that she sees lazing in the shadows on the hottest desert mornings.

She knows she gave up too much tonight, that things will be awkward with Gordon from now on, but that's okay. There's nothing permanent anymore. There's nothing that says this life has to be lived waiting for the next shame. "Natalya is not coming back," Tania says aloud, and then she says it again and again and again, until her words have lost all shape in her ears, until she feels something rise up inside her, a sense of confidence, of lucidity, that she can't recall ever possessing. She sits down in the white plastic chair and realizes that what she's feeling, after so long, after all these years, is relief.

# Living Room

A week after Joanne and the kids disappear, I call Del, my older brother, and ask him to come by to give me a quote on some contracting and design work I want done.

"This doesn't sound like something my firm would normally do," Del says.

"It's a simple redesign," I say. "Move a couple walls. Bring in some furniture. What's so hard about that?"

"I'm not even sure what you want is legal, strictly speaking," Del says.

"It's not *illegal*," I say, "strictly speaking."

I'm sitting in my den and looking out the window to the empty street of my gated community. There are seven homes on my cul-de-sac and in the three years I've lived here, I've never met a single other owner. We wave at each other as we pass, certainly, and there was the time one realtor murdered another realtor in the empty house on the corner and we all gathered on the hot asphalt to watch the coroner wheel out the dead body and fancy gold jacket of Century 21er Rhonda Lefcout, a woman I'd wished dead every time a new calendar with her face appeared on my doorstep, and to whose smile I jerked off once when our wireless Internet went on the fritz, but never once have I had an actual conversation with any of them. There's no tragedy in this. I value my privacy more than I value a conversation about the heat, or the cold, or the disposition of the HOA's discretionary fund.

"Look, Jason," Del says, "I'm happy to meet up and have a few beers with you, talk about the kids, whatever, but I have to advise you that you're asking for a lawsuit here."

"I don't intend to open the house to the public," I say. I hear Del sigh, and I know that I have him. "How does tomorrow at noon look?"

"This is going to be expensive," Del says. "Those espresso machines alone run to several thousand dollars."

"What price happiness?" I say.

Outside, a man and his standard poodle drive by in a golf cart, just as they do every day at 1:00 PM. Where they go—and why—is a mystery, but I know that by 1:30 they will be back, and by 1:45 the man will stand on his front lawn, standard poodle beside him, and he will chip imaginary golf balls out of an imaginary bunker. I find this very odd since we actually live on a golf course, one filled with real golf balls and real bunkers.

After a while, Del says, "How's Joanne?"

"Gone the way of the large reptiles," I say.

"Oh, Christ, man, I'm sorry. What happened?"

"I'm not entirely certain," I say, which is true. One day she and the kids were here, and one day they were not. The kids weren't mine; Joanne brought them into the relationship like she brought in the duvet covers, stemware, and Meg Ryan DVDs. "Maybe there will be an article in *US Magazine* and it will all be clear."

Three years ago, after getting a rather choice divorce settlement from my first wife, I moved to the desert in hopes of finding the personal freedom I thought I deserved. Carolyn and I had met in college and survived several calamities together: my failing out of law school; my failing out of the MBA program; my decision to invest my remaining student loan money into an auction website that was supposed to be just as good as eBay, but which turned out to be nothing like eBay at all, particularly since it was operated by Filipino gangsters and not Republicans; the death of both of our parents; the death of our desire to have sex with each other, that sort of thing. What finally broke us, however, was my decision to go into the pharmaceutical sales industry, which was made easier since Carolyn was a doctor and employed me as her office manager. We had boxes and boxes of prescription pads. Carolyn, bless her heart, thought that I made a poor business choice. The last thing she said to me, after our divorce was finalized, was "I'd appreciate it if you'd make an effort to stay out of prison."

And yet: a gate, a guard, an elaborate system of laser locks, night vision cameras, and a guaranteed armed response are at the touch of my fingertips. Joanne, before becoming my second wife, was my real estate agent. She wasn't like Rhonda Lefcout, however. She never left calendars for anyone. She said that calendars only made people aware of how long they were really tethered to their homes.

"I like what you've done with the place," Del says. He's standing in the living room, where I took the liberty of taking a claw hammer to the mirrored wet bar and have done some minor reconstruction on a curio cabinet filled with framed wedding photos.

"Mirrors and cabinets aren't the flavor I want here," I say. "I envision this area will have several two tops, three sofas, four or five of those overstuffed chairs in blue or black. I'd even be happy with leather if you wish to deviate a smidgen."

Del steps through the living room and then walks down the long hallway which leads to the kids' bedrooms. I follow behind him as he peers into each room. I don't know what he expects to find. I've already cleaned them out and have begun reimagining them. I'll need plenty of dry storage space, I know that. Plus, I'm required to have at least one large walk-in refrigerator to keep the pastries, the three different kinds of coffee cake, the new freshly made sandwiches and all the Frappuccino mix and whipped cream chilled. I've already begun transitioning the den into a break room.

"Jason," Del says, quietly, "I can't be a part of this."

"You're the only person I trust," I say.

"You have no reason to trust me," Del says.

"But I don't blame you for anything, either," I say. "That makes you an exclusive party in my life."

Del cracks open what was once the cedar-lined hall closet where Joanne kept her furs. I've already filled it up with napkins, cup sleeves, straws, and stacks of Bruce Springsteen, Al Green, Joan Baez, and Alanis Morrisette CDs.

"What happened to you?" Del says.

Nothing just happens.

It takes a week, but a member of the HOA's architectural committee finally shows up. Though Del has not been working in the house himself, he's hired a staff of twenty men and women to do the job, working in alternating twelve-hour shifts all day long. I've been sleeping in the backyard in a tent, and, in hopes of not annoying the workers too much, I've taken to urinating on my putting green and defecating into the fountain Joanne installed in our courtyard. The gentleman from the HOA catches me just as I'm zipping up on the green.

"Pardon me," he says, "but are you the owner of this home?"

"I am," I say. I'm not sure I know this man. He looks familiar to me, but I'm not sure I can accurately place him, so I decide that he might be one of those nameless people I see in my dreams, the neurological character actors who look on while I fuck realtors or jump off skyscrapers or eat handfuls of sand on the moon.

"Yes," he says. "Well. It appears you're doing some renovations. Would that be correct?"

"That would."

"Yes. Well. You see, you haven't filed the proper paperwork with the Association, and the bylaws clearly state that before any architectural improvements can take place that paperwork must be filed in a timely manner."

Two of the workers—Chet and Vince I call them, though I don't actually know their real names, my sense being that if I'm paying them to work, I can call them whatever I choose for the twelve hours they're in my home—come outside with a stack of blueprints and lay them across a sawhorse. This concerns me. Chet and Vince aren't part of the design team. They are strictly movers and shakers and lift-with-your-legs men.

"Is there a fine?" I say.

"Yes," the man says. "And I'm going to need your work to cease immediately."

"That's not possible," I say. Chet and Vince are twisting the blueprints around in circles, and I hear Vince say something about Del indicating the need for recessed lighting near the periodical stacks and that they're gonna have to rewire the whole fucking garage.

"Is it my understanding that people are working here twenty-four hours a day?"

"How could I ever possibly know what you understand?" I say.

Before the man from the HOA can respond, the UPS truck pulls up for its daily drop-off and half of my staff piles out of the house to help bring in the delivery. Today it's the sofas, the flip-top glass refrigeration unit, twenty crates of beans, and a set of uniforms.

"What are you building?" the man asks.

"A Starbucks," I say. The UPS truck hauls away, and out on the street I see the golf cart and standard poodle both waiting patiently for their master. I look at my watch. It is exactly 1:00 PM.

"That's against the CCRs."

When Joanne and her kids—were there two or three of them? I can't seem to remember now—moved in, she demanded to read the CCRs. When I asked her why, she said that she wanted to know which rule to break first, because she wanted to be the kind of neighbor other people gossiped about, or else she'd go crazy living on a golf course guarded by fat men with guns. "Normal people don't live in vacation homes," she said. That night and for the next 1,094 nights, she parked her car on the driveway, left the garage door open whenever she felt it prudent, and cheated her way toward the Ladies Bunco Tournament title. Someone loved the pilgrim soul in her. I loved the charlatan and the grifter.

There were three kids. I'm almost certain of it.

"Let me ask you a question," I say. "Do you remember seeing any kids living here?"

"Sir, I'm sorry if this is a bad time for you," the man says, "but you must understand that we all live here to avoid just this sort of willy-nilly construction. Don't you like living here? Isn't it beautiful?"

"There were two girls," I say. "I know that much, but I'm not sure if I'm confusing one of them with Joanne. So there might have been one girl and one boy. It seems like it's right there on the tip of my tongue. You ever get that? Sort of like a sense of perfect clarity, and then you just can't wrap your mind around it? You ever get that? Like when you're outside *pretending* to play fucking golf when there's a golf course in your fucking backyard? Or when you and that genetic fucking mishap of a dog go out for your thirty-minute battery-powered drive? You ever get the feeling that absolute truth is one fucking imaginary golf swing or thrilling bit of bestiality away? You ever get that?"

The man looks at me for a long time without speaking. Not hours or minutes or even really seconds, but like he's frozen in front of me and time is stopped, and I'm the only one who is still aware that time should be moving and people should not be frozen.

"Yes. Well," the man says. "I do hope you're not considering a drive-thru or any kind of amplified music."

I interviewed fifteen candidates but finally settled on Zack. He had the most prior experience and seemed to understand the project the best. Plus, there were never any ice particles in his Frappuccinos and his mochas were always double pumped.

"You understand that you'll be expected to live here," I say. We're sitting across from each other in overstuffed chairs, the *New York Times* spread between us, Al Green singing about times being good and bad, happy and sad at a reasonable volume through the house speakers, and two pieces of crumble coffee cake have been placed discreetly on perfect white plates. My living room has never looked better.

"You got it, buddy," Zack says.

"Eventually we'll get you a few co-workers," I say. "Maybe even a woman. Maybe two or three. But the first month is a probationary period, you understand, just to make sure it's a good fit."

"Whatever it takes," Zack says. "That's my philosophy."

"Refreshing," I say. "When can you start?"

"When would you like me to start?"

I like Zack. He's a smart kid. Though I guess I'm not sure if he's actually a kid. He could be thirty. He could be nineteen. He has a goatee and floppy hair, and he wears a leather necklace with an interesting pendant around his neck. He has a very discreet tattoo of a sunburst on his left forearm. He smells vaguely like patchouli, which I find comforting.

"Now sounds good," I say.

"Well, all right," Zack says, rising. I stand up as well, and Zack shakes my hand vigorously. "Let me just get set up behind the counter, and we'll get it going for you."

"How much time do you need?"

Zack runs a hand through his mop of hair and exhales through his mouth like he's really contemplating. "Give me ten minutes," he says.

I head off to my bedroom and place a call to Del. I've kept my bedroom fully functional in the belief that everyone needs a haven, even if home is paradise. God had the Garden of Eden, after all, and as I lay on my bed waiting for Del to pick up, I believe his only mistake was not eating the apple Himself.

Del answers on the tenth ring.

"Hello Jason," he says.

"I'm calling to invite you over," I say. "I'm having a soft opening this afternoon."

"I'm not free today," he says.

"Well, then I'll have a soft opening tomorrow, too," I say.

"Is there any reason why Joanne's mother would call me?" he asks.

"Joanne?"

"Your wife, Jason," Del says. "Your wife. You remember her, right?"

From the living room I can hear the sounds of milk being frothed and Bruce Springsteen doing an acoustic take on "Born To Run." Zack has changed CDs, which is fine. A little advanced warning would be nice, but that's why it's a soft opening.

"Are you there?" Del asks.

"Yes," I say. "Joanne. Lovely woman. And all of her kids. They were simply divine little creatures. All four of them. Three of them. Whatever, right?"

Del clears his throat, and I wonder what took him so long to answer the phone. Ten rings! Who doesn't have voice mail that picks up after four? Was he standing there staring at his caller ID and just counting? Did he decide ten rings was an appropriate number of rings for his only brother to sit through?

"Jason," Del says, "listen. Joanne's mother is worried. She hasn't heard from her in over a month."

"That makes two of us."

"She says you won't pick up the phone when she calls."

"I'm a very busy man," I say. "Do you know how much time goes into opening a Starbucks franchise? They don't just pop up overnight. And let's talk about not picking up the phone. You let the phone ring ten times yourself, so don't go running around passing judgment on people, all right? Ten rings equals inconsiderate. Terrible customer service. Someone ought to rewrite your company's handbook, Del. It could be a systemic problem."

"Please, Jason," Del says, but I hang up before he can finish his sentence. No one is going to ruin my first day of business. Not Del. Not Joanne. Not Joanne's mother. Not ten goddamned rings. Nothing.

Zack greets me with a broad smile when I step into the living room. He's casually wiping off the counter with a damp white towel. "Hey, bud, how you doing today?"

"I'm fine, thanks," I say.

"Great day out there today, huh?"

"Yes," I say. "Top five all time."

Zack chuckles and shakes his head. "Man, I was just saying that. Top. Five. All. Time! Hey, is there something I can get started for you?"

I crane my neck back and stare at the menu affixed to the wall. "I'll have a, uh, venti double-pump mocha," I say.

"You want that hot?"

"Always," I say.

"Always," Zack says, nodding. "Can I get you a pastry? Maybe one of our new brownies?"

"Crumble coffee cake."

"You gonna eat that here?"

"Always," I say.

"Always," he says. "Cool. Can I get your name, bud?"

"Jason," I say, and Zack scribbles it on the side of my cup.

"All right, that's $5.01, Jason."

I hand him six dollars and tell him to keep the change. "Always," I say.

"Let me get that order right up for you, bud," Zack says, and then he fires off one of his smiles again, and I think that he looks familiar to me. Like Joanne's son. Or maybe her daughter. The one I liked, anyway. It doesn't matter, I suppose, because Zack is happening now.

After two weeks, Zack and I begin to understand each other's rhythms. I'm not a morning person, so Zack figures out that he doesn't have to be at work at 6:00 AM. He can sit in the casita I had built for him and do whatever it is he does until ten, at least, but he's usually up and doing side-work by nine. I allow him to close at 8:00 PM as caffeine after 8:00 PM usually gives me insomnia, and insomnia is not a condition I especially need right now. If friends are coming over, not that they have, or if I think I'd like a fruit and cheese plate or an apple caramel bar after hours, he'll leave the pastry fridge unlocked. It is my house, but I like Zack to feel like he has his own workspace. I know how important being your own boss is, and I wouldn't want to make Zack feel like he's being watched in his own office—even if I were watching him, which I am. Today, however, has been rather trying. The guard at the front gate keeps calling to inform me I have guests who want to come in, despite the fact that I've told him I'm not expecting guests. He tells me that these aren't invited guests, that they are men in uniforms, and that they're fairly adamant in their desire to see me. I tell the security guard that unless they have a warrant or a battering ram, I'm not interested in entertaining this afternoon.

I decide to go out for a cup of coffee, see if I can't sort through this issue.

"Hey, bud," Zack says when he sees me in the doorway. "How's it going today?"

"Fine," I say.

"Fine? That's awesome."

"Yes," I say. "Everything is fine. The world is fine. The air is fine. The stars, the fucking moon, the fucking sun, all the pieces of dull cutlery in every dirty kitchen drawer, frozen yogurt, toasted sandwiches, all of it is fine."

Zack tosses his hair back and gives me a grim nod of the head. "I've been there, bud," he says. "I'm beginning to think that life doesn't really hold the same meaning for me that it used to. Some days, seriously, I wake up and it's a wonder I don't hang myself with dental floss."

"Would that work?"

"Oh, yeah," Zack says. "Sure, sure. You have to wind it up some. Really get it into almost like a rope, but that stuff is tough. It'll slice right through your skin, sever a couple arteries, and then you're just chum for the flies."

"That sounds painful," I say.

"Well," Zack says, "it sure isn't the way to enlightenment, but it'll get you to that next stage eventually. Hey, is there something I can get started for you?"

I give him my order and for a while I just watch him work the espresso machine. He's a fine boy, really, lots of energy and panache. At night he often leaves the house and meets a friend named Skylar for a drink. She's a pretty girl, nice teeth, a tattoo on the small of her back, also of a sunburst, oddly. Zack has had her over for dinner a few times. They'll barbeque steaks on the small grill he has on his patio, and then they'll sit outside talking or laughing or not speaking at all. She spent the night yesterday, and when I woke up in the morning I saw her out in my garden, stooping to smell the roses Joanne planted last season, only now fully in bloom. I wonder if Zack would like me to hire her for the second shift. I wonder if she has another friend, perhaps a girl slightly older, someone without any tattoos, who might be interested in working on the weekends. It would require more casitas. Or not.

"Here you go," Zack says, handing me my venti double-pump mocha and a piece of crumble coffee cake in the center of a white plate. "You have a great day, Jason."

"Tell me something," I say. "Do you have a family?"

"Everyone has a family," Zack says. "Am I right, or am I right?" He turns his back to me and begins wiping off the counter around the espresso machine with a damp white towel. "You have a good one, now, okay?"

"Sklyar seems nice," I say.

Zack stops cleaning the counter and slowly turns to face me. "Excuse me?"

"Sklyar," I say. "The woman with the tattoo on her back. The woman who spent the night last night. The woman who was outside this morning smelling my roses. Skylar."

If I met Joanne today, I imagine she might look a bit like this Skylar. Though I suppose women have always looked the same, it's the clothes and the body ink and the scars that change them. That and children. You keep another human inside you for nine months, and I think it's fair to assume you might leave the experience slightly different. It's such an alien thing: a beast that grows inside you until it crawls out bloody and screaming. If sperm came out of men like angry rainbow trout hooked through the lip, I believe we'd be less cavalier about the whole subject matter. I imagine Skylar might be the kind of woman who wouldn't want to be invaded in such a way. Zack is lucky to have her.

"I need to go on my lunch," Zack says abruptly. "Is that all right?"

"I've offended you," I say. "I didn't mean to."

"No, no, you haven't offended me," Zack says, but I can tell he's lying. You don't practice medicine—or at least pretend to practice medicine—without being able to spot obvious self-delusion. "No worries at all, bud."

"I'd like to make you permanent," I say. "I'd like to wave the next two weeks of probation. I'd like to give you a raise and begin paying for your medical insurance. I'd like to do that now."

"Sure," Zack says. He undoes his apron and sets it on the counter, locks the register, and turns off the light inside the pastry display. I grab a copy of the *New York Times* and sit down in one of the overstuffed chairs and pretend to drink my coffee while Zack turns off the machines. "Do you want me to keep the interior lights on?" he asks. I look up but don't see him, so he must be in the back.

"Please," I say.

"What about the CD?"

"Yes, please. I'd be happy to hear the Rolling Stones rarities," I say. "Or Lucinda Williams. Either one would be fine."

Zack doesn't reply, but a few moments later I hear the opening strains of Lucinda Williams singing about changing the locks on her front door. I try to get invested in a front page story about the president ordering the torture of some prisoners, but it's impossible. I know that I've offended Zack, and it makes me heartsick in a way I haven't felt since ... well ... since the last time I felt heartsick. Almost two months now.

"All right," Zack says. He's standing by the front door dressed in his non-work clothes: jeans, a T-shirt fashioned with an iron-on of Clifford the Big Red Dog, an LA Dodgers baseball cap. "Good-bye."

"You have a great day," I say, and just when I'm about to add his name to the salutation, it completely escapes my memory. So instead I say, "bud."

When Zack doesn't show back up after seven hours, I decide to slip into his casita to see if he's sick or if he's fallen in the shower or if he's hanging by a noose made of dental floss. But all I find is his tightly made bed. He didn't even bother to leave a note with a forwarding address. Just like that, he is gone forever.

You never get used to people disappearing. It's not the lack of closure precisely, but the sense that perhaps you've played a role you weren't aware of initially. With Joanne and the kids, the signs were there: the packing; the airline tickets to Hawaii, Australia, and Burma purchased on my credit card; the strange way Joanne kept telling me to stay the fuck away from her or she'd call the police; the way she called the police; the way she and her three kids (I'm almost certain there were three of them now—I've counted the bedrooms and it makes sense) were here one night and then that next morning they weren't. I remember waking up and feeling like the house was listing to one side and that the living room was about to crack in half. Something had to be done, obviously.

I spread out on Zack's bed and close my eyes. I imagine I am Zack. I imagine that woman I saw in my garden this morning, the woman with the sunburst on her back, is above me and that she is leaning down and whispering into my ear. I want to imagine she is Joanne, but I can't conjure her face, can't smell her skin, can't quite tell myself what it is I'm doing at all, if any of this is happening. Because if you think about it, it's all a little preposterous that I've turned my house into a Starbucks, but the facts of life are that we only get to live for a small amount of time—I mean really *live*, not that diaper period on both ends of the spectrum, or the acne era, or any time when life gets broken up by making photocopies, or sitting in meetings, or listening to music in elevators, or shopping for groceries, or waiting for that certain someone special. How much real time is that? Maybe 1,095 days. Maybe. And anyway, this living I'm doing inside the house now feels moored and solid.

Tomorrow, I decide, I will put an ad in the paper for a new employee. Or wife.

Part of being a good boss, I've learned reading the Starbucks franchise handbook, is an ability to perform all of the remedial tasks you expect of your underlings. Corporately it's referred to as the reverse plane-crash theory. I prefer to think that it's simple survival instinct, though I suspect I'd have a difficult time killing a wild boar or skinning a cougar if it came down to it. Working for Carolyn, I learned a great deal about medicine, or at least which drugs people really wanted, which ones made people happy, which ones made people angry, which ones made people irrational and suspicious of the black helicopters. So that when a patient would call and Carolyn was busy, I'd occasionally dispense my own diagnoses and even call in prescriptions, though the majority of my business was handled outside of the office, certainly. I would have been an excellent doctor, and I am sure many people believed I was one.

Del, of course, always knew the truth. He always knows. So when he shows up at my front door the day after my full page want ad runs in the *Los Angeles Times*, *Chicago Tribune*, and *USA Today*, I fire up the espresso machine to show him how much *I* know.

"What can I get for you?" I ask.

"I'm not here for coffee, Jason," he says.

"No charge," I say.

"Fine," Del says. He looks up at the menu, and I can tell he is impressed. Unlike most Starbucks, I have all the seasonal drinks available year-round. "Just give me a latte."

"Nonfat? Whole milk? Soy? Eggnog?"

"Jason, look, it doesn't matter."

"It does to me," I say.

"Fine. Nonfat."

"Great," I say. "Can I get you a pastry or something? I even have the classic coffee cake. No one has that. I challenge you to find it anywhere else."

"Yes, fine, that would be fine."

"Great," I say. "Why don't you have a seat, and I'll call your name when your drink is ready."

"Jason," Del says, "have you heard from your wife?"

"Take a seat, *sir*," I say, "and I will call you when your drink is ready. Please, help yourself to a *New York Times*. They are complimentary."

Del ignores the newspaper but takes a seat on the blue crushed velvet sofa and stares out the window to the street. From the way the shadows bounce on the walls I can tell that there is some activity outside, but since it is just after 1:00 PM, it may well be that man and his enormous poodle. Or maybe that woman with the sunburst has come over to have a cup of coffee. Maybe Joanne and the kids have returned. I would welcome that, truly, because the house has started to sag at the corners again. The casita in the back is nearly gone entirely.

"Venti latte on the bar for Del!" I call out. Del stands up carefully, and I note that the tilting of the house is really becoming pronounced. I'm amazed Del can actually walk without pitching downhill toward me, but he makes it to the counter without any problem.

"I want you to listen to me," Del says.

"You have a great day," I respond, sliding Del his cup.

"Joanne's mother has gone to the police. They want to come in and take a look around. No one is saying you've done anything, Jason, okay? They just want to look around. Will you let them do that?"

"Zack is missing," I say. "So is the girl with the sunburst."

"Skylar," Del says.

"Yes," I say, "that was her name. She came around quite a bit, and then when Zack left, well, I guess it became uncomfortable for her. She liked Joanne's roses. I saw her outside smelling them one morning."

"Jason," he says, "we've been through this before. I want to help you, but you have to let me. The police just want to talk to you. That's all."

"You have helped me," I say. "I couldn't have accomplished everything here without your help. Have you taken photos for your portfolio? I can't imagine that I'm the only person in America who wants a Starbucks in their house. I saw on MTV that Tommy Lee has a very small one, but he also has a stripper pole, which I think is excessive. It's about comfort and customer service, and you've really accomplished that. I just can't get any decent help."

Del rubs at his eyes with the palms of his hands. When we were kids, our mother admonished Del to never do that, because she said it led to bags under the eyes, loose skin on the cheeks, and a general hangdog appearance. It never stopped him, and I'm proud to say he looks nothing like a hangdog.

"Zack and Skylar have been dead for two years," Del says. "You need to wrap your mind around that."

"Have you noticed," I ask, "how the house seems to be sagging?"

"Are you hearing me, Jason?"

"Perhaps I should just have my bedroom removed. I've found that I spend most of my time in here anyway."

"In five minutes," Del says, "a police officer is going to come to the front door, and I'm going to let him in. You'll have two options then: you can tell him where Joanne is or you can go to jail, and if you go to jail, they're going to want to ask you questions that you're not going to want to answer. They'll talk to Carolyn eventually, which will then lead to other questions about things you've lied about. Do you want that, Jason?"

"She's in Burma by now," I say.

"Good," Del says. "Now we're getting somewhere. What is she doing in Burma?"

I tell Del all about the fighting, the plane tickets, the calls already placed to the police. I tell him that sometimes people you love disappear and that, through no fault of your own, they stay gone. And sometimes they reappear. I tell him that Zack and Skylar certainly are not dead, that they were both here not a week ago, and that after they left, that's when I noticed things really starting to get weird around here with the foundation of the house. I tell him that I might move. I tell him that I might just try to get back into medicine. I tell him to get the orders from the men at the door, to find out if they want hot drinks or cold, if they would like pastries, if they would like to take a seat while I get busy making them whatever they'd like. And when Del steps away from the counter to open the door, I tell him to have a great, great day.

# The Models

It's midnight and Terry Green is parked in front of the entrance to Sawtooth Mills, a new gated community in Scottsdale that boasts "325 planned homes in five luxurious models." In the backseat of his Ford Explorer, Terry's two young children, Seth and Liza, are asleep. He looks at them in the rearview mirror and tries to remember the night each was conceived. With Seth, he's pretty sure it was the night he came home from work early, surprising his wife, Polly, with a bouquet of roses, a bottle of red wine, and tickets to *Cats*. God, how Polly loved that Andrew Lloyd Webber crap. She used to listen to the soundtrack from *Joseph and the Amazing Technicolor Dreamcoat* like those kids in lowered Hondas bumped rap music: the bass turned thick and dusty, the treble just a hint in the background. They did it right there on the kitchen floor. He remembers walking to the bathroom to clean up and finding an old Cheerio stuck to his ass. Seven years later and he still can't recall a single box of Cheerios ever consumed in his home. The Case of the Immaculate Breakfast Cereal, Polly called it.

About Liza, well, that's more difficult. Terry has always tried not to think about the specifics. Why burden yourself with all that shit? There's no choice. Your wife is pregnant, you take responsibility. Terry conjures the perfect instance that might have created his cherished five-year-old daughter. He pictures a perfect Sunday morning. He imagines sunlight filtering through plantation shutters and casting slim shadows over their entirely white and blue denim bedroom. Polly wakes him with a subtle kiss on the lips and then rolls over on top of him, the ringlets of her hair hanging over her naked breasts. They make slow, passionate love to each other, their bodies in perfect sync. And when they are finished, they walk hand in hand to the kitchen. They drink orange juice out of glass mugs. They read the *New York Times*, sharing a laugh over the crossword puzzle question that always seems to appear each Sunday—*Spanish Gold*—and then they make love again on top of the *New York Times*, their bodies damp with newsprint when they're done.

And maybe that's how it happened, Terry thinks. He hopes, really. Liza should be the product of love and not whatever emotion he and Polly devolved into.

Terry reaches under the passenger seat and pulls out the bolt cutters, then steps out of the car quietly so as not to wake the kids. It's their first night in Arizona, and Terry thinks he might like to live here one day. He likes the way the stars look in the dense heat of summer. They remind him of a piece of blown glass Polly won at a parking-lot carnival in Walnut Creek. Back when they were kids. It was black with specs of gold and silver and white, and at night, in Polly's bedroom, they'd place a flashlight behind it, and the entire room would become the Milky Way. What were they then? Sixteen? Seventeen? It should have just stopped right then. One night, one of them should have just said, "Enough," and then they would have gone on to different lives. They would see each other at a high school reunion, and maybe they'd feel a pang of regret for what was, or what could have been, or what they told themselves they'd never be.

There's a three-inch-thick padlock on the gate to Sawtooth Mills, but the developers or on-site realtors haven't bothered to lock it. Developers and realtors are very trusting people. How many must get murdered every year? He checks his watch and figures they have eight hours, tops, before they'll need to be back on the road. Nine hours if they really want to press it, but after what happened yesterday in Las Vegas, Terry knows he can't settle for mistakes. He's never thought of himself as a violent man, but the more time he's spent running, the more he's envisioned hurting people who stand in his way. His mother used to tell him that what you let your mind dwell on, you become, though Terry never believed that particularly. Nevertheless, Terry thinks that he'd prefer not to be one of those men who get used to the sight of blood. That's a choice. That's something you can control.

Terry shoves the gate open a few feet, enough for his SUV to squeeze through, and then slips back into the driver's seat. He looks in the rearview mirror and sees that Seth has stirred awake.

"Where are we?" Seth says, his voice dripping with sleep. Terry has been keeping the kids calm by giving them sips from a bottle of cherry-flavored codeine cough syrup he found in a sales office in Winnemucca.

"Home for the night," Terry says.

"Real home or fake home?" Seth says.

Terry thinks about just turning the car around and heading for the police station in Phoenix. He thinks about dropping the kids off with a note that says he's sorry, that he didn't mean to do anything wrong—but the one thing he can't reconcile with that scenario is that he doesn't feel sorry. To feel sorry would be to admit that there was a choice in the matter, and that, Terry knows, is simply not the case.

"Fake home," he says.

After putting both kids to bed—Seth in the football-themed room, with the life-sized poster of Peyton Manning and his offensive line standing guard over the football-shaped bed like Christ and his disciples (except Christ never looked so alive, at least not in Terry's opinion), and Liza in the Strawberry Shortcake room, its walls covered in pink wallpaper, dozens of stuffed animals and dolls perched comfortably atop the bed—Terry goes back out to the front gate and locks the padlock, figuring that alone will buy them extra time if they need it.

What a perfect neighborhood this will be, Terry thinks. The developers were sparing no expense, what with the redbrick walkways that spiral around the houses and head off toward the luxurious green spaces. He notices that instead of regular streetlights they've installed faux lanterns, like alongside Main Street at Disneyland, and that there are benches beneath every third one, alternating back and forth across the street. Terry imagines Seth and Liza riding their bikes down the street at dusk while he sits on one of the benches chatting with a neighbor.

It's likely that this neighbor would be about Terry's age and that sometimes they'd talk about work—Terry likes to think that he'd be a fireman in this new life and that his neighbor would be something a little less exciting, like a pharmacist or the owner of a sporting goods store—and that sometimes they'd talk about taking both of their families out to the river to ride Jet Skis to get to know each other a little better, seeing as they lived right on the same street, and that there might even come a time when they'd vacation in Hawaii together.

Terry wonders how long it has been since he's had a real conversation with another adult. Not a conversation about the weather, or about traffic, or about how he'd like his burger cooked, but about life, about dreams, about the future, about the past, about what happens when you wake up one morning and decide to kidnap your children and then can't undo the action, in fact don't even want to undo it, because your love is what they need in their lives right now—though of course you know you've fucked them up for the rest of their lives, that their potential for success as adults, their potential to live in a neighborhood just like this, shrinks with every passing second.

Once back inside the house—the sales flyer says that it's the Palmetto model, 2,500 square feet, four bedrooms, three baths, a great room, a den, a living room, and a pool-sized backyard for just $525,000!—Terry makes his way to the master bedroom and unfolds himself across the California King, flicks on the flat-screen television and watches the fuzz, and wishes (for not the first time) that life was simpler, like when he was a kid, when everyone got the same thirteen channels and that was fine. Who needed eight hundred channels of Food, HGTV, and Discovery? Wasn't it enough just to have the moving pictures tell a story? Wasn't it enough to have a cop, a robber, and a conclusion all in one hour?

The good won, the bad lost, and the credits ran. Who were the good guys and bad guys on the Food Network? All these *decisions*, Terry thinks, have made it nearly impossible to be bored anymore.

Terry figures that he spent half of his childhood bored. His mother worked across the bay in San Francisco, so each afternoon after elementary school he'd park himself in front of the TV at home to watch reruns of *The Monkees* and *Lost In Space* and *The Courtship of Eddie's Father*. He can't recall a single favorite episode of any of these programs, which he finds troubling. All that time he spent with Micky Dolenz and the Space Family Robinson and Bill Bixby and there's nothing he can conjure in his mind to fill the void of the snowing (handsomely wall mounted!) flat screen. What he does remember, though, is a sense of vacancy. What did he do for all those hours between when *The Courtship of Eddie's Father* ended and his mother came through the door carrying boxes of take-out Chinese? He knows that's when he began imagining what the people in the other houses on his court were doing, what they were eating, what shows they were watching, and sometimes he thought about sneaking into their houses to watch them, often going so far as to walk around the court peering into windows, inhaling the smells of cooking macaroni and cheese, catching the flickering blue image of local newsman Van Amburg, a man he considered, in retrospect, more of a parent figure to him than his own misplaced father.

Since all the houses on the court were exactly the same inside, save for the two-story model which was exactly the same only in the downstairs, Terry even knew where he'd hide if given the opportunity: beneath the stove-top was a huge cabinet that everyone kept their pots and pans in, but it was such a huge cabinet that it actually took a dogleg left toward the sink, creating a large cubby just big enough for a child to fit in. He could sit right there all night and no one would ever know.

His childhood is a period of time Terry recalls as being filled with a lingering sense of nausea, as if he were always on the precipice of retching, aware even then that something just wasn't *right* in his head. Normal kids don't think about peeping on other families. Normal kids don't suffer from ennui. Terry knows Seth and Liza will never have that problem.

He sets the alarm on his cell phone for 6:30 AM, though of course he knows he'll never sleep that late. He hasn't slept more than four hours in a night in nearly a month, but he can't be too careful, he can't get too comfortable, which is why he chooses to get back up and put his shoes on before finally closing his eyes.

Snatching Seth and Liza was remarkably easy. He called Polly and told her that he'd like to take the kids out to dinner so that she and her boyfriend, Landon, could have a quiet night to themselves. Originally, that was all he wanted to do, though as time has passed, Terry has come to believe that he's been priming himself for this kind of decisive action for years.

"Why are you being so nice?" Polly asked.

"Shouldn't we start acting like adults?" Terry said.

"That's your problem, Terry," she said. "You've always acted like an adult. That's what ended it, you know."

What really ended it, Terry knew, had nothing to do with him being the responsible one in the relationship. What ended it was that Polly liked to fuck other men and that Terry let her. It wasn't an explicit agreement, of course, merely a decision made to practice avoidance. Terry understood that they'd married far too young, that their lives had somehow devolved into a Bruce Springsteen song, but that they had Seth to think about, and that meant Terry needed to let Polly do the things she needed to do. He was confident that after she spent some time fucking men who rode motorcycles, or who fixed motorcycles, or who simply dressed like they did either, she'd come back to him and their love would be stronger. He even considered buying a motorcycle at one point. He imagined showing up at the kindergarten she taught at wearing leather chaps, a studded vest, and sporting a Fu Manchu mustache, and she'd just hop on the back and they'd ride off, her co-workers lining the street to clap, whoop, and holler. Instead, he told Polly that he thought it would be great fun to spend the evening reading aloud to each other from *The Lord of the Rings*, figuring it would take a very long time for them to complete the trilogy and that, by the end, they'd feel like they'd accomplished something together and, maybe, Polly would stop fucking guys who rode motorcycles.

"You're right," Terry said.

"Well, anyway," Polly said. "The next girl might appreciate it, Terry. But spontaneity is good. Adventure is good. There's no reason you shouldn't get married again. I'm still very fond of you, if it's any consolation."

"I guess it will have to be," Terry said.

"Have you been dating?"

"Polly," Terry said, "this isn't something I want to talk about with you." The fact was he'd been out on a few dates recently, mostly with women he met on sales or service calls. He was a hero when he showed up in his suit and tie to fix the copy machine; yanking accordioned paper jams out from the broiling hot center, his hands covered in black ink. The women would rush to get him a glass of water or a wet towel to clean up with, and he'd be polite and thank them and smile. In an office, heroism is replacing toner and fixing the collator, but in real life, at the bar or restaurant or bedroom, when your life boils down to the fact that you are an expert at fixing a machine that merely replicates someone else's creativity, the insignificance can paralyze you. It can stop you from performing even the most mundane task. It can make people not call you back. Or not stay the night. Or just roll off of you midway through, remembering an appointment at 3:00 AM on a Wednesday

Every Hewlett Packard copier he sold had the equivalent of an airplane's black box in the center of it, tracking each and every movement of the machine. If need be, Terry could plug his laptop into it and replay weeks' worth of activity, every single copy that had been created, every jam, every nuance of the machine. With one keystroke, he could reset the machine to the moment before trouble had started, erasing all the activity, clearing the memory, restoring the machine's settings to what he thought of as the Nirvana Moment, when all things inside and out worked in perfect synchronicity.

His personal Nirvana Moment came a few weeks after Polly had given birth to Liza. Polly caught a vicious cold, and, for the sake of the baby, she went and stayed at her mother's house, leaving Terry at home alone with both children. He knew then that Liza wasn't his, but she was Polly's and that more than sufficed. For nearly a week it was just the three of them, and though at the time it seemed like just a small fraction of life, just an increment of existence, no more than maybe half a sheet of paper if life came in reams of five hundred sheets, Terry latched onto it and kept it apart from Polly. Whenever he felt at a loss for who he was, or about the dissolution of his marriage, or whatever failings he had as a father, he simply performed a system restore on his mind and returned to that week alone.

"You know what," Terry said. "I could take the kids for the whole weekend if you like. It would be no trouble."

"Really, Terry?" Polly said. "That would be so great. Landon's been bugging me for the last month about going to some B&B in Napa, but I didn't know how to ask you."

"Go," Terry said. "Have a great time."

"You are sweet," she said. "You know that, Terry, right? You were always sweet."

When Terry hung up, he wasn't precisely sure where he was going to take the kids, or even why he felt so strongly that it was the only way to save them from a life of replication, or even if he was actually going to take them anywhere at all. He'd have two days of lead time to make sense of it, and by then he was confident it would become clear. And if it didn't, well, he could just keep clicking that button in his mind, restoring things to a point more favorable.

Terry opens his eyes and checks his watch. It's 6:15 AM, exactly one hour since the last time he opened his eyes and checked his watch, and the only noise in the house is the faint hum of electricity. In the last month, Terry has begun to notice how much noise electricity makes. Minus major appliances and air-conditioning, most houses just have a faint, haunting din caused by plugged-in lamps and televisions, not even a sound so much as it is feeling, a magnetism not unlike the sensation Terry gets when he knows someone has just departed a room he's recently entered. During the first night Terry and the kids spent in a model home—a 1,900-square-foot two-story in a development called Manor Creek just east of Reno—he was constantly checking over his shoulder for other people, certain he felt someone staring at him, positive that he'd caught a whiff of cologne or perfume. He even went so far as to look inside the kitchen cabinets in case a child had found a cubby, but no one builds cabinets with that kind of depth anymore. Eventually, even the kids began to notice how different the empty houses sounded, so when he could, Terry would plug in the refrigerator, dishwasher, and the washing machine just for the electrical comfort they seemed to give the children.

This morning, though, the silence feels encouraging, especially in light of the fuck-up the previous morning in Las Vegas. They'd spent the night in a beautiful golf course home at a country club with three names—The Lakes at The Resort at Summerlin Commons—which Terry felt was the kind of home he'd live in after he retired. He could see himself playing gin rummy with the boys at the clubhouse, could see Seth and Liza and *their* spouses and *their* children sitting poolside, sipping drinks, tanning themselves. He'd fallen asleep that night on the plush leather sofa in the home's library and only woke up when he realized someone was shaking him. It was Seth.

"What's wrong?" Terry asked without opening his eyes.

"I can't find Liza," Seth said.

Terry spent the next three hours frantically searching the house and the surrounding golf course and vast grounds, sure that Liza had simply wandered off as small children sometimes do, but he was also equally plagued by the very real fear that she'd been kidnapped by some wacko pederast and was only moments from certain death. The country club was gated, so he was sure she couldn't have gone far, but a gate doesn't stop a psychopath from moving in.

Calling the police was the right thing to do, the only thing to do, but that just wasn't possible. How do you explain to the police that the child you kidnapped has been kidnapped?

Terry finally determined that the best thing to do was to simply sit with Seth in the living room of the home they'd spent the night in, just like anyone who was considering the home might, and see if Liza came wandering back through.

It was 9:30 at this point, and already prospective homeowners were piling through the six models named after famous golfers—Terry and the kids had spent the night in the Nicklaus without even considering the Trevino and Snead—and after giving Seth two big swigs of the codeine cough syrup to calm him down, Terry tried to relax by watching the touring families and imagining who they were, what they did for jobs, what their private secrets were; except that there weren't any families, just older couples who arrived in their Mercedes Benzes and Lexuses, and younger couples in Escalades. To each new couple, Terry said the same thing: "We don't come with the house."

No one laughed, which surprised Terry, until he realized how disconcerting it must be to walk into your future, only to find someone already inhabiting it.

As minute after minute passed, Terry began to grasp how little of his own future had been realized. What had he wanted as a child? What had he wanted most? His therapist told him that what he really wanted was a stable family, but Terry thought that was just the hourly rate talking, a good starting point to spend days and days dealing with his obvious Freudian anger. All Terry was certain of was that, at one time or another, he'd wanted to be *more*. More of *what* he did not know, but he was sure, sitting there with Seth snoring quietly across his lap, that he knew why humans were the only animals to keep pets: the opportunity to have both dominion and love without tangible responsibility. If you lose a dog it's a shame, but it's not a crime.

He imagined what Liza would be like in twenty years if he and Seth just picked up and left in ten minutes. Then in five minutes. And two minutes. Would her life be more? Would she achieve beyond what, Terry realized, was likely to be a prolonged descent into white trash servitude? If you get abducted by your own father—or at least the man who decided he was your father—what are the odds that you'll end up lecturing at Harvard on molecular biology versus the odds you'll end up stripping at a "gentlemen's club" in Portland, Oregon, the spit of some drunk trucker drying on your ass?

By the time he'd carried Seth out to the Explorer and set him in the front seat, Terry Green had decided that the long coil of Liza's life would be better held in someone else's hand, someone who wouldn't just let her disappear, or, worse, take her in the first place. And when he saw her there asleep in the backseat, still in the previous day's clothes, and realized he hadn't even bothered to bring her inside the night before, he couldn't decide if he felt relieved or disappointed.

Terry wakes Seth and Liza up at 7:00 with a handful of candy he's stolen from the sales office. He's already filled up the Explorer with the three pallets of bottled water he found in the garage of their overnight home, as well as a stack of frozen Lean Cuisines from the icebox inside the sales office, three Styrofoam take-out boxes from someplace called Thai Smile that smelled relatively fresh, as well as the office's small microwave. He's spent another ten minutes with a bottle of Windex wiping down the surfaces he and the kids touched in the model, but Terry knows this is probably overkill, especially since at least a hundred people have walked through the house over the course of the previous day. Still, Terry thinks, a decent person cleans up his own mess.

"Where are we going today?" Seth asks after he gobbles down a handful of M&Ms.

"California," Terry says. "Maybe New Mexico. Maybe Utah. Let's just get on the road and see where it ends." Terry is trying to sound cheery and fun, but he's aware that a weariness has crept into his voice, and he understands that eventually time and tide will catch up to him and neither will sweep him away. By now, Terry thinks, he must be national news. Liza and Seth are adorable. He is relatively handsome. There are photos of him and Seth in matching Little League uniforms. Liza even appeared in one of those baby beauty pageants. Christ. What were he and Polly thinking? It was long after that whole JonBenet shit, and yet they still did it, dressing her up like a fucking princess and taking her down to the Airport Marriott in Oakland so that she could lip synch to "I Will Always Love You." She didn't even place. What was she then? Three? He imagines Nancy Grace doing shows all about him. He imagines that alien-looking Greta Van Susteren interviewing his mother, his friends, his co-workers, the women he didn't sleep with.

"Can we go home?" Liza asks.

"No, no," Terry says. "We're still on vacation. Aren't you having fun on vacation? Isn't this neat?"

"I miss Mommy," Liza says.

"Me, too," Seth says.

Me three, Terry wants to say, though in fact he doesn't miss Polly as much as he misses some memory of Polly, though he can't say which one specifically. The weird thing, he knows, is that when he really presses for a concrete moment of their lives together, he normally ends up conjuring the baby powder smell of her deodorant, or the feeling her palm left on his back when she would absently place it there while they walked through Target looking for hand soap and his dandruff shampoo, or the strange ebullience he felt when her name popped up in his email in-box even after their divorce.

"Why don't we call Mommy when we get to the next city?" Terry says. "Maybe she and Landon are finally home. Would you like that? Maybe we'll do that."

In Quartzsite, just ahead of the Arizona border with California, Terry stops at the massive Flying J truck stop and pays an attendant twenty-five bucks to let the kids shower in the "trucker's only" shower stalls while Terry stands guard. After the kids get out, he'll plop them down inside the arcade for a few minutes while he looks for an Explorer whose license plate he can steal. He figures it will take them another eight hours to get back to the Bay Area. And then? You spend an entire lifetime thinking about who you're about to become, and then one day you realize who you are and nothing seems to line up exactly. Terry understands this to be true now, understands that if he wants to fight fires he'll have to beg to be placed in one of those programs where convicts get to fight the most dangerous, life threatening fires; understands that if he could find the little black box inside his head, he'd try to restore the system back to about 1989. Three days after graduation from high school and he and Polly and the entire just-graduated senior class of Northgate High School were on a cruise ship bound for Mexico. It was an absurd choice, this cruise, as Terry had never felt like he really fit in with the other kids. Oh, he'd had plenty of friends, had even been somewhat popular, had played varsity baseball, had been active in student council, had been one of the guys everyone liked, though it was clear he wasn't admired as such. Which was fine. But this cruise—a seven day affair—would be his undoing, he knew. Could he be trapped on this floating city of other people's lives without, just once, trying to slip into another room? It was all about proximity and opportunity, Terry understood, and he'd been able to quell his sneaking need around the neighborhood by simply getting to know his neighbors over the course of eighteen years. After having found reasons to enter all of the homes on his cul-de-sac—a cup of sugar for cookies was a general suburban need not even the childless neighbors could deny, he found—the allure had abated some. More and more often, however, entire city blocks began to spike his interest. What was going on in all those homes? What were the people he could see only as shadows against blinds saying to each other? What did their furniture look like? Were the beds against the wall or under the window? Who still had a black-and-white television that they actually used? Who used liquid detergent and who used powder? Who still used a wooden cutting board? Did the dogs get to sleep on the beds of the children? Did all the clocks have the same time on them? Did their VCRs blink 12:00? Would they even notice he was there? Could he live inside an inhabited house and never be found? Could he will himself invisible?

It was a test. Terry believed then that if he could spend seven days without breaking threshold, he could do anything. If he could not be himself, his true self, for seven straight days, it was reasonable to assume that he could assimilate into a life of normalcy, even if it meant living inside an alien skin.

Terry lasted five days, though he reasoned that it should have been expected that he'd sneak into Cooper Donovan's room, particularly since he had a fairly good idea that Polly was fucking him, too. And the fact that it was true—that she was indeed fucking him, and that he listened to it all from underneath the bed—made it all forgivable. Polly was drunk. Cooper was drunk. And that Polly tearfully told him all of it as they stood watching a famous Mexican blow hole, La Bufadora, gave him a sense of true validation. Other people's closed-door lives were just as sordid and disappointing as his own; even if the life belonged to the woman he loved.

So he decides his next move. He will take the children back. He will place them inside their beds while Polly and Landon sleep. He will hide his children in their own home, so that when they wake up they might just think it was all a terrible dream, that the last month spent sleeping in model homes across the West was a shared delusion. First, he'll take them to Lippert's ice cream parlor in Pleasant Hill, a place they used to go to as a family for birthday parties, and he will pour a healthy dose of cough syrup into their root beer floats. He'll use the key Seth wears around his neck to unlock the backdoor—he'll wait until at least 3:00 AM, until even the most fervent insomniac finally buckles under and takes an Ambien or Tylenol PM—and he'll carry Liza in first, to make sure, to not fuck it up again. He might sit for a moment alone with just Seth in the car, because Terry realizes that he's infected this poor seed of his with his own particular brand of sickness, just as he's sure someone infected him. His mother? His remarried-five-times father? You can blame your parents for only so much, Terry knows, but he imagines he'll spend a few final moments with Seth whispering directives into his ear on how to live a good life, that he'll be like Marlon Brando showing up to tell Christopher Reeve's Superman how to be Superman even though he'd died twenty-five years and eight thousand light years previous. And then he'd carry Seth into his bedroom, would tuck him in tight, would kiss him once on each cheek, would maybe cut a small lock of his hair off and keep it in a locket, something to look at while he drove across America. He figures that he might just get off, that it might be a gray area of the law if you kidnap your own children and then return them, particularly if you haven't done something awful to them along the way.

Then Terry notices how very quiet the Flying J truck stop has become, how very alone he is standing in the hallway outside the shower stalls, how clearly he can hear Seth and

Liza laughing and talking and splashing, when before all he could hear were the sounds of truckers and families pouring around him, their conversations meeting him in quick thrusts of language, the kinds of conversations he'd like to replicate sometime, conversations about going and coming, about getting somewhere, conversations he's imagined a million times. And in his mind, Terry Green begins to press the reset button over and over again, closing his eyes against the growing cacophony of sirens in the distance, tries to focus on the knock-knock joke he can hear his son telling his daughter (*Knock Knock. Who's there? Shirley. Shirley who? Shirley you know this joke.*), tries to make a choice, tries to find a reason, tries to keep it together just a moment longer, tries to tell his children, when they walk out and ask him what is going on, what is happening, Daddy tell us what's wrong, that everything is fine, that everything is going to be just fine, that everyone is going home.

# Granite City

They disappeared during the coldest winter on record. There was no special episode of *America's Most Wanted*. No jogger stumbled on a human skull. Instead, it was Scotch Thompson's bird dog, Scout, who came running down Yeach Mountain with a human hand in her mouth. And just like that, James Klein and his family were found.

"Damndest thing I ever seen," Lyle, my deputy, said. "All of them stacked up like Lincoln Logs. Like they were put down all gentle. Terrible, terrible thing." We were sitting in the front seat of my cruiser sipping coffee, both of us too old to be picking at the bones of an entire family, but resigned to doing it anyway. "You think it was someone from out of town, Morris?"

"Hard to say," I said. "It's been so damn long, you know, it could have been anybody."

James Klein, his wife Missy, and their twin sons, Andy and Tyler, fell off the earth sometime before October 12, 1998. Fred Lipton came over that day to borrow back his wrench set, but all he found was an empty house and a very hungry cat.

"You think it was some kinda drug thing, don't you?" Lyle said, but I didn't respond. "You always thought Klein was involved in something illegal, I know, but I thought they were good people."

"I don't know what I think anymore, Lyle," I said. A team of forensic specialists from the capital was coming down the side of the mountain, and I spotted Miller Descent out in front, his hands filled with plastic evidence bags. I'd worked with Miller before and knew this wasn't a good sign. What Scout the collie had stumbled onto was a shallow grave filled with four bodies, along with many of their limbs. The twins, Andy and Tyler, were missing their feet. James and Missy were without hands.

Miller motioned me out of the cruiser. "Lotta shit up there," he said. Miller was a tall man, his face sharp and angular, with long green eyes. He had a look about him that said he couldn't be shocked anymore; that the world was too sour of a place for him. "Like some kinda damned ritual took place. Animal bones are mixed up in that grave, I think. Need to get an anthropologist up here to be sure, but it looks like dog bones mostly. Maybe a cat or two. Snow pack kept those bodies pretty fresh."

"Jesus," I said. "What's the medical examiner say?"

Miller screwed his face up into a knot, his nose almost even with his eyes. "Can I be honest with you, Sheriff Drew?"

"Sure, Miller."

"Your ME about threw up when she saw all them bodies," he said. "You know, I was in Vietnam so this doesn't mean so much to me. I've seen things that'd make your skin *run*, but she just, well, I think she was a little bothered by the whole thing. You might want to have them bodies cut up by some more patient people upstate."

"I'll keep that in mind," I said.

Miller smiled then and scratched at something on his neck. "Anyway," he said. "You still playing softball in that beer league?"

I never knew how to handle Miller Descent. He could be holding a human head in one hand and a Coors in the other and it wouldn't faze him.

"Not this year," I said.

"Too bad," he said, and then he shuffled his way back up Yeach.

I didn't get home that night until well past ten o'clock. I brewed myself a pot of coffee and sat at the kitchen table looking over notes I'd written when the Kleins first disappeared, plus the new photos shot up on the mountain. Since my second wife, Margaret, died, I'd taken to staying up late at night; I'd read or watch TV or go over old cases, anything to keep me from crawling into that lonely bed. But that night, my trouble was not with the memory of a woman who I loved for the last thirty years of my life, or my first wife, Katherine, whose own death at twenty-four still haunted me, but for a family I had barely known.

The Kleins moved into Granite City during the fall of 1995. James Klein was a pharmacist, so when he and his wife purchased Dickey Fine's Rexall Drug Store downtown, everyone figured it was going to be a good match. Dickey had gotten old, and going to him for a prescription was often more dangerous than just fighting whatever ailment you had on faith and good humor.

James and Missy were in the store together most days. James wore a starched white lab coat even though it wasn't really required. It inspired confidence in the people, I think, to get their drugs from someone who looked like a doctor. Missy always looked radiant, no matter the season, standing behind the counter smiling and chatting up the townspeople and, when skiing season started, the tourists who'd come in for directions or cold medicine.

All that to say I never trusted them. I'd known the family only casually, but I knew them well enough to know that they were hiding something. James sported a diploma from Harvard inside the pharmacy, and Missy looked like the type of woman who was best suited for clambakes at Pebble Beach. They were not small town people—they drove a gold Lexus and a convertible Jaguar—and Granite City is a small town. I never had cause to investigate the Kleins, never even pulled them over for speeding, but I aimed to at some point, just so that I could look James in the eye when I had the upper hand, when my authority might cause his veneer to smudge. That chance didn't come.

I picked up a photo from the gravesite, and there was James Klein's face staring up at me. Miller was right: the bodies had been well preserved by the snow pack. The skin on James's face was tight and tugged at the bones. His eyes had vanished over the course of the year and a half—eaten by bugs or simply by the act of decay—but I could still picture the way they narrowed whenever he saw me.

His body lay face up, his arms flung to either side of him. He was draped on top of his wife, his hands chopped from his arms, wearing his now drab gray lab coat. Shards of bone jutted from underneath his sleeves, and I thought that whoever had done this to him had taken great pains to make him suffer.

For a long time I stared at James Klein and wondered what it would be like to know that you were about to die. Andy and Tyler, the twins, must have known all too well that their time on Earth was ending before it ever had a chance to begin. They were only twelve.

I stood up, stretched my arms above my head, and paced in the kitchen while I tried to gather my thoughts. After the family had initially disappeared, I'd searched their home with Deputy Nixon and Deputy Person. We didn't find any forced entry or signs of a struggle, but we did find bundles of cash hidden in nearly every crevice of the house. All told, there was close to half a million dollars stashed in shoeboxes, suitcases, and file cabinets. The money was tested for trace residues of cocaine, heroin, and marijuana but came up empty.

For almost three months, we searched for the Klein family. In time, though, winter dropped in full force and even James Klein's own mother and father returned to their hometown. I told them not to worry, that we would find their son and his wife and their twin grandsons, but I knew that they were dead. I knew because there was $500,000 sitting in my office unclaimed, and no man alive would leave that money on purpose. And so, as the months drifted away and my thoughts of the Klein family withered and died in my mind, I figured that one day when I was retired someone would find them somewhere.

"Hell," I said, sitting back down at the kitchen table. My eyes fixed on a pair of pale blue Nikes, unattached to legs, pointing out from the bottom of the grave. I wanted to just sit there and cry for those boys, but I knew it wouldn't do either of us any good.

I got to the medical examiner's office late that next morning, figuring I didn't need to see her slicing and dicing. But it turned out I was right on time. The ME, a young kid named

Lizzie DiGiangreco, had been working in Granite City for just over a year. Her father, Dr. Louis DiGiangreco, had been ME in Granite City for a lifetime and had practically trained Lizzie from birth. She went to medical school back East and then moved home after her father died at sixty-four from heart failure. I was one of Louis's pallbearers, and I remember watching Lizzie stiffen at the site of her father in his open casket. I knew then that her profession had not been a pleasant choice for her, but that she was duty bound.

Lizzie greeted me with a handshake just outside the door to her lab.

"Glad you could make it, Sheriff," Lizzie said, only half sarcastically.

"Miller said you were a little queasy up on Yeach," I said. "I can get someone else to do this, if you want."

Lizzie made a clicking sound in her throat, a tendency her father displayed when he was about to be very angry, and then exhaled deeply. "I don't like to see kids like that," she said. "Maybe Miller is used to it, but I'm not."

"Understandable," I said and then followed her into the lab.

The four bodies were covered with black plastic blankets and lined up across the length of the room. Lizzie's assistant—what they call a diener—an old black man named Hawkins, was busy gathering up the tools they would need for the procedure. I'd watched a lot of autopsies in my thirty-five years as sheriff in Granite City, but it never got any easier. Hawkins had been Lizzie's father's assistant, so he knew what I'd need to make it through the next few hours.

"There's a tub of Vicks behind you in that cabinet, Sheriff," Hawkins said. "These folks ain't gonna smell so fresh."

Lizzie glared at Hawkins, but she knew that he didn't mean any harm. Hawkins could probably perform an autopsy just as well as she could, and Lord knows he never went to medical school.

Hawkins pulled back the first blanket, and there was James Klein's naked, handless, body.

"Where'd you put the hands, Hawkins?" Lizzie asked.

"I got 'em in the jar by the back sink," he said. "You want them now?"

"No," she said. "But make sure not to cross them up with Mrs. Klein's."

Hawkins nodded in the affirmative, and I was struck by how, for these two people, this was a day in the office. For Lizzie, maybe, seeing those children would be different. But for Hawkins, they would be nothing but cargo, something to load onto a table and then something to haul back to the refrigerator.

Lizzie sliced James Klein with a Y incision, starting from his shoulder, across his chest, around his navel, and down through the pelvis using a scalpel. The room filled with a smell like raw lamb. It was the muscle tissue, the meat.

For the next two hours, Lizzie spoke quietly and clinically into a tape recorder, noting the condition of James Klein's vital organs as she examined and weighed them. I had to leave the room only twice: when Hawkins sifted through the intestines and when Lizzie and Hawkins peeled back the top of James Klein's head and removed his brain.

After they'd removed all of James Klein's vital organs, his corpse sat opened on the examining table: his trunk resembled the hull of a ship under construction. Both Lizzie and Hawkins were covered in blood and tissue.

"Well," Hawkins said to me, "he's dead all right."

"Why don't you go get a cup of coffee, Hawkins," Lizzie said. "The sheriff and I need to go over a few things before we sew up."

Hawkins licked at his lips then, and I saw that his hands were shaking a bit. "I don't know what it is," he said, "but doing these things damn near starves me! You want something, Doc?"

"No, Hawkins," she said, and when he was gone, she started back up. "Off the record, because I'll need to look at the tox screens and some of the neuro X-rays, but I'd say the cause of death for Mr. Klein was suffocation plus blood loss from his hands being chopped off."

"Suffocation?"

"Look here," Lizzie said, pointing at James Klein's lungs. "He had severe hemorrhaging, probably caused by inhaling so much dirt, and there's bruising along the back of his neck. See that?"

There was a dark purple bruise along the base of James Klein's neck, but what was odd was the shape of the bruise. It was a pattern of small squares.

"What do you make of those marks?"

"Probably the bottom of a work boot or hiking boot," Lizzie said. "Like someone was standing on his neck, pushing his face into the dirt, while they cut off his hands."

"Using his head for leverage," I said, not as a question, and not really to Lizzie, but to myself. Said it because I had to hear myself say it.

Lizzie nodded, and I saw that she was looking over my shoulder at the bodies of the two boys. "Yeah," she said finally, her gaze averted back to James Klein, "that's probably what happened."

"All right," I said. "How long will it take you to finish the rest of these up?"

Lizzie exhaled so that her bangs fluttered in the air for a moment. "About two hours for each of them."

"Okay," I said. "The families are flying in this afternoon. Can you get me something preliminary on paper tonight?"

"I'll try," Lizzie said, and then both of us were silent for a minute.

"I miss your dad," I said, because at that moment I really did. We'd been good friends for many years, and when he died I knew that the old school in Granite City was getting close to recess time. "He was a good man, Lizzie. I'm sure proud of the way you've stuck around here, and I know he would be, too."

Before Lizzie could reply, Hawkins walked in with a Danish in his teeth and two cups of coffee. As I walked out, Hawkins and Lizzie started dumping James Klein's internal organs back into his body in no particular order.

Just after noon, a helicopter containing James Klein's mother and father, plus Missy Klein's mother, a Mrs. Pellet, landed on the football field at Granite City High School. Lyle and I were there waiting for it.

"I'm real sorry about this," I said to Mrs. Klein when I shook her hand.

"You said you'd find him," she said.

Before I could answer Mrs. Klein, before I could tell her that we'd found him just as I knew we would, her husband placed a hand on her shoulder and directed her away from me.

"This is a hard time for her," he said, and then he, too, was gone, squiring his wife into the back of a rented Aerostar we'd brought for them. Mr. Klein wore a houndstooth sport coat that hung off his shoulders like a dead vine and a pair of expensive sunglasses that day. I knew that behind those tinted glasses were the eyes of a man without hope. I'd seen that look on the face of every man who'd lost a son.

Lyle helped Missy's mother off the helicopter, and I could tell that, like Mr. Klein, she was face-to-face with the dead end of life. She was older than I'd remembered her from the months she'd spent in town, but I guess waiting for bad news would do that to you.

We drove the three of them to the Best Western on Central, none of us speaking until we arrived there.

"When do we get to see them?" Mr. Klein asked. We were waiting for the elevator to take the Kleins and Mrs. Pellet up to their rooms.

"Tomorrow, I'd guess," I said.

"We'll want to bury them in Connecticut," Mr. Klein said, and Missy's mother, Mrs. Pellet, nodded in agreement.

"That's fine," I said. "The medical examiner still needs to finish getting some information though."

"For what?" Mr. Klein said. "So that we can be told my son suffered? I don't need to know any more to understand that he's gone. That all of them are gone."

"It's a murder investigation," I said. We'd told both families that their loved ones had been found, though not the condition of their bodies. Foul play, we'd told them, was suspected. "There are procedures that must be followed. I'm sorry if you have to stay here one minute longer than you want to, but this is my job, and I'm planning on doing it."

"Sheriff Drew," Mr. Klein said, "do you have any children?"

"I don't."

"I know my son wasn't a good person," Mr. Klein said. "My wife and I have reconciled that much. He was a drug addict and probably a pretty good one, if you want to know. He was also a gifted liar. I am sure he made enemies in many parts of the world or else why would he come to a place like this?" Mr. Klein swallowed, and it seemed then that he was at some point, that he'd figured out a troubling problem that had always been just within reach. "So, you see, Sheriff, I don't need to know who did what. I don't need that kind of element in my life. I'd prefer to think that my son was the decent person he pretended to be."

"I'll keep that in mind," I said.

"Sheriff," Mrs. Pellet said, her voice soft and tired, "I just want to bring my baby home. Whoever killed her, if anyone did, is gone. If you haven't found who did this yet, you never will."

"She's right, you know," Lyle said as we walked back to our van. "They're both right, sort of. We went through every lead we had on this case over a year ago, Morris."

"But there's all kinds of new technology, Lyle," I said. "There's a national database of violent crimes, advances in science. DNA. We can try, can't we?"

Lyle reached into his pocket and pulled out a pack of Lucky Strikes and lit one. I'd known Lyle for half my life, and he'd always been someone I could depend on. He wasn't what you might call book smart, but he knew things instinctively like no one I'd ever known, before or since. "Tell you what," he said, smoke drifting out of his nose in smooth wisps of gray. "I get cable just like you. I see all those forensic shows on Discovery and I think they're fantastic. I'm glad the cops in LA are solving crimes from the 1950s using space shuttle technology. But you know what, Morris? *This ain't LA.*"

He was right, of course, which made it all the more difficult to take.

I was sitting at the counter of Lolly's Diner eating meatloaf and reading the autopsies of the Klein family when Miller Descent walked in and sat down next to me. It was near nine o'clock.

"Lyle said you might be here," Miller said.

"Just reading about that family," I said, holding up the autopsy report. "And trying to swallow some food. Can hardly do either."

Miller chuckled and then paused. "I wanna ask you something, Sheriff," he said cautiously, "and I don't want to offend you in any way by asking it."

"That's a tough order now." Lolly came by then to refill my coffee cup, and Miller asked if he could have a slice of apple pie. "Well," I said when Lolly left, "spit it out."

"Do you think maybe you should turn this case over to someone else?" Miller said.

"That doesn't sound like a question, Miller," I said. "It sounds like a request."

"Assistant DA upstate saw some of the crime scene pictures," Miller said. There was a sheepish quality about him then that I wasn't used to, and I realized that this wasn't something he was enjoying. "I probably shouldn't have shown him a damn thing, but you know how favors work around up there, right Sheriff?"

"I guess."

"Well, he thinks this is something the Brawton police, maybe the homicide unit they got out there should get involved with, or at least maybe a more . . ." Miller trailed off when Lolly dropped his pie off. "Hell," he said. "You know what I'm trying to say here, right? Talk to the family, let them know it's an option."

What he was trying to say was that there was some glamour to this case: *Wealthy young family found murdered in ski hamlet downstate. $500,000 sitting in evidence room gathering dust.* And glamour means an assistant DA upstate becomes DA, or mayor, or worse—a congressman.

I also think Miller was trying to say that I didn't have a chance in hell of finding a killer and that maybe I should let the blame fall on somebody upstairs.

"Yeah," I said. "I understand."

Miller sat there and ate his slice of pie in silence after that, never once asking to see the autopsy file wedged between us.

"All right then," Miller said, standing up to leave, his plate cleaned of all remnants of apple pie.

"Don't you want to know how they died, Miller?"

Miller stuffed his hands into his pockets and sort of bowed, biting his bottom lip hard until it looked painful, and then shook his head from side to side. "This is what I know about these things," Miller said. "There ain't a cause or an effect once they've started to rot and such. They're dead and they're not coming back. If they were meant to still be alive, if God wanted them here right now, then goddamn it, they'd be here. Time's up, that's all."

"You're wrong," I said, suddenly angry with Miller, angry with the DA who wanted a big city detective to run this case, angry with my wife Margaret for dying three years ago and leaving me alone. "There is cause and effect, Miller. People don't just punch in and punch out. Kids died up there, Miller. *Kids.* You can't apply your mumbo jumbo to them. No one deserves that. You know what? You're wrong, Miller. This isn't about rotting bodies and old bones. You can't just toss a blanket over every body you see and pretend that they aren't *someone.* Do you know that Miller? Do you know?"

Miller frowned at me and started backing toward the door. "Acute hemorrhaging of the lungs, and occulation of the blood vessels around the eyes and face, suggesting suffocation. General failure of the major organs due to severe blood loss and the ensuing shock," Miller said. The words tumbled out of his mouth like he was reading from a textbook. "Wounds consistent with a number of drug related murders in a hundred different towns that aren't Granite City. I'm sorry, Sheriff," he said. "I really am."

I watched Miller climb into his car, a beat-up El Camino, and drive off. I knew then that I didn't want to end up like Miller Descent: a hard man unable to shake the horrors from his mind. I also knew that I was halfway there and closing the gap. So, with an envelope filled with the pictures of a dissected family in my hand, I left Lolly's Diner and headed home, where I knew what I had to do, and where I knew I would not sleep.

Mr. and Mrs. Klein and Mrs. Pellet were sitting in the lobby of the police station when I came in the next morning. It was chilly that day, and I remember thinking that maybe winter wasn't over, that Yeach Mountain might once again get a coat of snow. And I thought, seeing Mr. Klein in his linen pants and his crème-colored polo shirt, that maybe my time in Granite City was coming to a close; that I couldn't bear to see despair in people's faces anymore. That, most of all, I couldn't keep on thinking about the daily rituals that still call to people even in their times of need: the soft pleat ironed down Mrs. Klein's pant leg, the way Mrs. Pellet had put on a nice dress and gold earrings.

"Been waiting long?" I asked.

"No," Mr. Klein said. His voice was low, and I decided that he probably wasn't long for this place either. "Didn't get much in the way of rest last night."

"I've got the autopsies for your son's family," I said. "You can read 'em if you want to."

Mrs. Klein let out a short sob and squeezed her husband's arm. Mr. Klein kissed her on the forehead and patted her hand. "Did he suffer, Sheriff?" Mrs. Klein asked.

"No," I said. "No, it looks like he died peacefully."

"What about my Missy?" Mrs. Pellet asked. "And the kids. What about the kids?"

"The same," I said. "I think they got lost in the woods is all. A real tragedy." A look of relief passed over their faces, and though I believe they each knew that their children and grandchildren had died terribly, that in fact they'd been butchered, I had helped them in some way. Had eased something in them for at least a moment.

Lyle walked out then and tapped me on the shoulder. "Dr. DiGiangreco called for you," he said. "Needs you to call her right away."

I told the families to wait for just a little bit longer and I'd get the bodies of their loved ones released. Lyle followed me back to my office.

"What the hell's going on out there?" Lyle said. "I thought I heard you tell them their kids died peacefully."

"I did," I said.

"Morris," Lyle said, "their damn hands and feet were cut off!"

"I know that," I said.

"Lizzie said some DA called her," Lyle said. "You aware of that?"

I opened the door to my office and let Lyle stand in the hall. "You talk to your kids lately, Lyle?"

"You know, Morris, when I can," Lyle said. "Why?"

"How about you take today off and drive down and see your daughter," I said. "Shoot, take the whole week off. Fly out to California and see your son. When was the last time you saw him?"

Lyle squinted his eyes at me and rolled his tongue against his cheek. "Whatever this is, Morris," he said, "I hope you know what you're doing."

Lizzie answered on the first ring. "They're all wrapped up and ready to go," she said.

"How do they look?" I asked.

I heard Lizzie sigh on the other end of the line. "I had to use fishing line to sew the boys' feet back on; Hawkins had some thirty-five-pound test that worked great," she said. "It should hold for a long time."

"I appreciate this Lizzie," I said. "More than you'll ever know."

"What do you want me to do about this DA who keeps calling?"

"Tell him to call me if he has any questions," I said. "The family hasn't asked for anything and it's not his case."

"You've got all the paperwork there?" Lizzie asked.

"Right in front of me," I said. "I'll sign off on it and get you a copy."

"Would my dad have done this?" Lizzie asked.

"I don't know," I said. "I don't know if you should have."

"Hawkins said that if there was a problem he'd take the blame," Lizzie said. "Said that's how it's always worked here in Granite City. 'Let the shit roll downhill,' were his exact words."

I thought then that my recollections of Lizzie's father had grown opaque in my mind—my memories colored more for what I wished was always true than what actually was. We'd worked together for a long time, and time spares no one.

"Tell Hawkins I won't forget this," I said.

"Sheriff," Lizzie said, "can I ask you a question?"

"Sure."

"Why'd you stay here all these years?"

After we hung up, I pulled out a piece of letterhead and scratched out a three-sentence letter of resignation. I held it in my hands and ran my fingers over every word, every period. I'd been the sheriff of Granite City for thirty-five years, and I'd never broken the law.

I always did the legitimate thing, like telling men who beat their wives that they were going to hell when I didn't even believe in God, and then letting them go on back home because the law said we couldn't hold them. Like knocking on poor Gina Morrow's door at three o'clock in the morning to tell her that her husband had been stabbed to death in a bar fight over another woman.

I'd always followed the letter of the law, no matter my opinion of it. What good did it do? Couldn't I have lied to Gina Morrow and told her that her husband had been stabbed to death trying to protect an innocent woman's honor? Couldn't I have dragged some of those no-good wife beaters out behind the station and pounded them into submission, beaten them until they begged me to kill them?

And yet, there I was with my letter of resignation in my hand and an autopsy report on my desk. Inside both documents were lies. Inside the autopsy report, Dr. Lizzie DiGiangreco, whose dead father I had carried to his grave, stated that all four members of the Klein family had died of exposure and acute hypothermia. She further stated that all members of the family were fully intact—that all hands and feet were connected. An accidental death, no note of foul play.

In my official report, typed the night previous on my old Olivetti, I stated that it was my belief that the Klein family had succumbed during the night of October 10, 1998. The almanac noted October 10, 1998 as being the coldest day of the month during the coldest winter on record. Over a foot of snow fell that night.

Case closed.

Snow did fall in Granite City the night I quit, and though the roads were slick and runny, I called Lyle and asked him to meet me at Shake's Bar. We sat for a long time in a small booth sipping beer and eating stale nuts. That next day I'd recommend to the mayor that Lyle be named interim sheriff, a post he would eventually keep for three years until he died from emphysema.

"You know what, Morris?" Lyle said. "I've been thinking a lot about just closing up shop and moving to Hawaii. You know I was stationed out there, right?"

"Yeah," I said.

"In those days, I raised a lot of hell," Lyle said. He had a faraway look in his eyes, and I thought maybe inside his head he was on liberty in Maui. "I don't regret it, though. We all had to sow our oats at some point. Make bad decisions and then just close those chapters and move on."

"I never really did that," I said. "I've loved two women in my life, Lyle, and both of them are dead now. From day one, I've tried to do right. What has it gotten me?"

Lyle took a sip of beer and then coughed wetly. "I know that, Morris," he said. "You did right by everyone, Morris. By everyone."

Lyle took a final pull from his beer and stood up.

"You heading home?" I asked.

"Naw," he said. "I thought I'd just take a drive through the streets; make sure no one's stuck in the snow. You could positively die from the cold out there tonight."

There was a twinkle in Lyle's eye then, and I knew that he had seen my report, had seen Lizzie's autopsy report, and that he didn't care. That he knew I'd made a judgment call not based on the nuts and bolts of the law, but on how people feel inside, on the mechanics of the human heart.

"I'll come with you," I said.

# Will

Richard expected that there would be a will reading, that somebody would call him a few days ahead of time—enough time, at least, for him to wrangle a decent pair of shoes for the event—with directions to one of those skyscrapers with reflective windows and orders on protocol. *Don't look anyone in the eye. Refer to everyone as sir. Do not wear jeans.* It was the clothing aspect that had Richard most worried. Here he was, thirty-five years old, and he'd lost the ability to dress appropriately. Having money again would change that, Richard was certain, and if that meant feeling uncomfortable for one more afternoon, well, that was a length Richard was willing to go.

He even knew how the event would go down, more or less. He'd be ushered into a room lined with dark oak walls and walnut cabinets, and a man wearing an ascot would pull out a high-backed leather chair for him to sit in. The man in the ascot, who'd have a British accent, would say something like, "I am so very bloody sorry for your loss, lad; my own father's heart was weak, too," and would leave him be for a few minutes. Richard would sit there in the austere office and he'd try not to laugh. When was the last time he actually *saw* his father? 1992? He'd remember breaking into the house in

1995, but he wouldn't dwell on that. He'd remember stealing his father's Benz in 2002, but, again, why dwell? No, he'd just keep real calm, and when the lawyers or servants or strippers brought in the bags of cash he was inheriting, well, then he'd celebrate, catch a plane to Vegas, and start living, finally.

That's how Richard figured it would happen. He even let his mustache grow so that, if need be, he could pluck out hairs from above his lip to produce tears or staunch smiles. So when the doorbell rang on the last Thursday of January and through the peephole he saw the same motherfucker who served him six months ago waiting with another envelope, he didn't even bother to open the door.

"Get a real job, you fucking jackal," Richard said through the door.

"It's not like that this time," the man said.

Richard knew that process servers were just normal people trying to make rent and feed their families, but it still rankled him that they should earn their livelihoods on his human suffering, even if his suffering was largely self-imposed. The last time this particular process server came for a visit he handed Richard a temporary restraining order from his own twin sister, Amy. Apparently, you call your twin sister a stupid cunt who doesn't deserve the air she breathes and then you accidentally set her hair on fire when you flick your butt at her, the State of California views that as paramount to a death threat.

That Amy actually *did* die in a car accident a few weeks before the hearing was no recompense to Richard. He didn't want her dead. Hell, he loved her, loved the memories of her he still had, the ones that lived inside of old pictures of the two of them in footsy pajamas and Rick Springfield songs and the smell of freshly cooked pretzels smothered in mustard. And there was the larger, genetic ache that still woke him up in the night; a kind of welling pain that felt like someone was trying to push all of his internal organs up into his chest. Somewhere along the line, things in Richard's life had simply turned to shit. That little boy with the twin sister dancing to "Jessie's Girl" had turned into the kind of guy that process servers remember explicitly, and though Richard couldn't pinpoint the exact date of this shift, he nonetheless realized that, at thirty-five, with no family left and with no one who actually loved him more than they loved his car or his sofa or his ability to steal identities off the of the Internet for a fee, shit had to change. Shit had to get better. Shit had to stop being shit.

"Whatever you got," Richard said, "I don't need."

"You don't even have to sign for it," he said.

Richard trolled through his mental Rolodex to see if there was anything he actually had pending legally and the fact was, since his sister's and father's passing, he'd felt it important to actually *try*. That was his buzzword: *Try*. *Try* to be good. *Try* not to fuck up. *Try* to do honor to the family name, though Richard truly never knew what that meant, apart from not embarrassing the dead, which seemed a ludicrous proposal; but in the wake of being the last living American branch of the Charsten tree, even Richard had to admit there was some psychic weight to it now.

When Richard finally opened the door he noted that the process server actually recoiled, and, for not the first time, he wondered when it was that people figured out he wasn't someone you wanted to be terribly close to. Even if the process server was lying, well, he was going to *try* to be understanding of the world and let him do what he needed to do without violence or threats or spitting.

"Okay," Richard said. "Here I am. Let's get this done."

The process server handed Richard a thick manila envelope that bore the watermark of one of his father's numerous companies, this one the law firm that bore his name, and for a moment Richard got the same nauseous feeling he always got when he saw his father's name in print, be it in the newspaper or on the Internet, as if his father's name actually possessed eyes and could see Richard.

The process server was already walking away when Richard called out to him. "That's it? Just this? Nothing else?"

"Your lucky day," the process server said.

Luck, Richard Charsten III knew, was fickle. In his life, Richard reasoned that most of his luck had been inordinately bad, resulting, most likely, from being born into tremendous good. His father, Richard Charsten II, was a lawyer of such means that he eventually decided that owning baseball teams would be a decent hobby to occupy his down time, just like owning multinational shipping companies once had, and, before that, tinkering around with a small start-up coffee company in Seattle which still bore his nickname, Deuce's, twenty years and fifteen hundred franchises later.

For the first seventeen years of his life, Richard basked in the remarkable luck of his birthright, knowing with perfect certainty that no matter how poorly he did in school, his father's money was as firm as bedrock. There was the house in Maui, the house in Aspen, the house in Paris, the house in Los Angeles he actually considered home, and the house in New York that was only used to impress politicians and free-agent ball players. There were the glossy debutantes who always had the best intentions and lowest expectations of him, which he met with gusto, and there was even a small circle of other would-be heirs that he considered true friends, though that turned out not to be true once his circumstances changed. It seemed then to Richard that he'd turn eighteen and would simply matriculate into a better party at some red-brick university in the East for four years before taking a token post in one of Deuce's companies. Life would continue in all its lavish glory until he eventually died of the clap or liver disease or another less enervating side effect of the good life.

He didn't expect to be kicked out on his ass. But then Deuce probably hadn't expected Richard to steal his credit cards, to crash three of his cars, to deal coke out of his home, to break into one of his offices in Los Angeles and throw a party. In retrospect, Richard understood why his father kicked him out, respected him for it even, because it takes a man to realize that his own son doesn't measure up. Back then, though, Richard didn't expect that he'd wake up on the morning of his eighteenth birthday to the sight of three men in Bekins shirts boxing his shit up. He didn't expect that the next seventeen years would be punctuated by stints at four different community colleges, nearly three aggregate years locked up for various felonious acts, and two ex-wives, one whom he actually loved and one who actually loved him.

His twin sister, Amy, had been his lone champion

most of those years, handling his cases, loaning him money, eventually even buying him his small apartment in Burbank so that he'd always have a place to live, even if he didn't have the money to pay for electricity or water service. What Richard never could comprehend was why Amy hadn't warned him about what was coming that morning of his eighteenth birthday, since he was sure she knew, because she'd always been the family consigliere.

The last time he saw Amy alive—the day he set her hair on fire—she'd just gotten him off with a small fine and time served for stealing the toner carriage out of a copy machine at Kinko's, an important element needed in a counterfeit check scam he was working.

"I really appreciate your help," Richard said. "That was a tight one." They were sitting on a bench outside the courthouse in Van Nuys. It was November, a few weeks before Thanksgiving, and the air was damp and cold. Days like this always reminded Richard of being in Paris with Amy when they were kids, acting crazy in the streets surrounding Sacre Coeur, him already high at age twelve or thirteen, hanging out with artists and hash heads, acting cool; Amy just happy to watch out for him, the two of them such different species. Shit. *Van Nuys. Like Paris in November.* That was the kinda shit that made him steal.

"How did it feel sitting in County for two weeks for ink?" Amy said. "Ink. Unreal."

"It wasn't my fault," Richard began, but Amy cut him off before he could finish.

"You know, you'll be forty in five years, and you still act like everything just shines right off of you."

"I said thank you," Richard said, standing up. He dug into his pocket and found a pack of smokes, lit one up and started walking away. This was a conversation they'd had before, and Richard knew enough that he didn't want to have it again, especially since they had it at twenty-five and thirty as well. It was like a five-year warranty that expired directly after particularly stupid crimes.

"No," Amy said, calling after him, "you didn't say thank you. You said you appreciated my help. There's a difference."

Richard turned back and faced his sister then, startled to see she was near tears. "What do you want me to do, Amy?"

"Stop fucking up," she said. "Stop being such a fuckup."

He'd meant to flick his cigarette in resignation. He'd meant to flick it and walk off wordlessly, holding firm to the last bits of dignity he thought he possessed. Instead, standing there, he finally figured it out. Amy hadn't told him what was coming that morning seventeen years earlier because she thought he deserved it. No. No. *Needed* it. And what good had come?

So he told his sister to stop being such a fucking cunt, to stop hogging all of the air with her sanctimonious bullshit, because better people deserved to breathe and that she should fuck off . . . and then he flicked his cigarette, and it landed in her hair, and now, three months later, he was sitting at his kitchen table needing her more than ever.

Spread out before Richard was the final will and testament of his dead father, Richard "Deuce" Charsten II, former owner of the Seattle Mariners, former shipping magnate, former coffee impresario; former living, breathing, cocksucker who booted his lone son out on his ass at eighteen in order to for his boy to "earn it on his own." The good news,

Richard saw, was that he was the rightful heir to approximately $250 million dollars, plus property and stock interests that nearly doubled that amount. Unfortunately, in order to claim his money, he'd need to handle one small bit of business in the next ten days that, Richard realized in sinking horror, was simply not possible. It was right there in plain legal English:

> *I give the rest of my estate (called my residuary estate) to my wife, Lenore. If she does not survive me, I give my residuary estate to those of my children who survive me, in equal shares, to be divided among them and any descendants of a deceased child of mine, to take their ancestor's share per stirpes. The following must be observed for my funeral and burial for the estate to be honored as such:*
>
> *1. My body must be cremated within forty-eight hours of my death.*
> *2. No autopsy must be performed unless required by the law of the land.*
> *3. My ashes must be distributed along the first base line of the Seattle Kingdome within ten days upon the issuance of probate.*

It heartened Richard that his father was so irresponsible that he actually failed to update his will since the death of Richard's mother in 1996, though Richard figured old Deuce probably imagined he'd live forever and that the will was just something perfunctory to appease some estate planner in his firm.

The more pressing issue was that the Seattle Kingdome, in an act of tremendous grace, was imploded in 2000. From the outside, the Kingdome had looked vaguely space age— like a standing set from *Logan's Run* had impregnated Space Mountain—but the inside was positively disco, right down to the hideous artificial turf that was basically cement covered with green fabric. Richard still had a scar on the small of his back from trying to slide on it in 1981, when he'd served as the Mariners' batboy over the course of his tenth summer. It would have been fun if the players hadn't hated his father so much, though not many other kids or adults could say they'd been spit on by men enshrined in the Baseball Hall of Fame.

Reverie aside, Richard was smart enough to realize this was a big fucking problem. The idea of possessing his father's ashes for any length of time was troubling enough, but the proviso that they be dumped inside the Kingdome was beginning to make him sweat behind his knees.

Well, he decided, he'd just do the right thing and call the person in charge, see what could be done, see if there was a deal to be made, *try* to make this work out well for everyone. He flipped to the front of the packet and reread the cover letter, which was, it seemed, a rather simple bit of correspondence signed by a lawyer named Calvin Woods. Richard pictured in his mind the kind of person Calvin Woods might be: probably about Richard's age, probably of a similar caste (at least initially), and now probably just as dissatisfied with his life as Richard was. If there was one certainty Richard picked up during the last seventeen years, it was that everyone wanted something better or, alternately, everyone wanted something less so that they could get home at a decent hour, kick off their shoes, watch *American Idol*, and fall asleep on their own schedule.

Calvin Woods would be a reasonable man, would understand the predicament Richard faced and make it right. And didn't Richard deserve a little grace here?

After rolling through a series of receptionists and secretaries, Calvin Woods finally answered the phone in the way all lawyers seemed to these days, by announcing his own name as a greeting: "Calvin Woods."

"Yes," Richard said, "hello. This is Richard Charsten. How are you today?"

"I'm fine, Mr. Charsten," Calvin said. Richard noted a definite lilt in his voice that indicated a level of annoyance. "I presume you received your father's will today."

"Yes, yes," Richard said. For some reason, Richard felt like he was being examined and recorded, which immediately sent him into what he considered his Upper Crust Mode, where he was all apologies and thank-yous and practiced civility, all staples of a previous life. "So sorry to bother you on this, Calvin," he said. "But I noticed a trivial issue here in the will that I thought we could rectify if you have just a moment of free time."

"I presume you're speaking of the Kingdome clause," Calvin said.

"Yes, yes, thank you," Richard said. The sound of his own voice was beginning to grate on Richard, the false civility, the undue thanks. He wasn't really sure where this persona came from as he sure as fuck couldn't remember his father thanking anyone for anything, while his mother was more the kind who expected people to thank her for her mere presence on Earth, as if being a socialite was some kind of ordained position.

"Well," Calvin said, "I'm afraid there's not much that can be done. Your father went back over his will shortly after your sister died and didn't make any changes. What you see is what he wanted."

"You're not hearing me," Richard said, and for the first time, he thought he actually heard his real voice pinging in his head. "That shit is my birthright, okay? That shit is mine by the word of the fucking law. He blew up the Kingdome himself. I saw him flip the ignition on ESPN. Why would he want his ashes spread somewhere that didn't exist? Okay? Why would he keep that in his will unless he was, you know, temporarily insane or something? You hear what I'm saying?"

"Maybe," Calvin said, "he didn't want you to get the money, Mr. Charsten."

Cruelty, Richard understood, after he called Calvin Woods an ass-fucking cocksucker and hung up on his uppity ass, wasn't an activity born out of necessity, but out of benign indifference: other people simply weren't as important. It was a lesson Richard learned in community college, jail, and marriage but which never failed to rearrange the way he looked at the world. It was true that Richard had, on occasion, felt the same way in the process of stealing identities or stealing cars or stealing the contents of an entire home from some Beverly Hills asshole (and Richard made sure of this: he didn't steal from people worse off than himself), but with the simple proviso that people of better circumstances were the non-important ones. And yet, he felt like even in death Deuce was sticking it to him. And for what? Not being Amy? Not being Trey to his Deuce? There was something else, though, some hope that this Calvin character simply didn't know what he was talking about. If Deuce didn't want Richard to have the money *now*, he certainly hadn't wanted him to have it in 1996, either. Or any of the intervening years, so why not correct the fucking thing to say that Richard was out all together? No, that money was his.

It took Richard a full day to come to grips with the possibilities attached to the station in life he was primed to lose yet again. It wasn't just the $250 million dollars—Richard was confident even he couldn't screw up $250 million dollars—it was the minutia of other valuables now in his name, provided he could turn up a domed baseball stadium sometime in the next nine days. Of most interest to Richard was his father's childhood home in Sarasota, Florida.

He couldn't remember ever stepping foot in the home, his grandparents having died when he was just a toddler, but merely seeing the address evoked a kind of muted sadness. Whenever Deuce wanted to prove a point to Richard (never to Amy as Amy pretty much sharpened points as her life's work) he'd drag out a crinkled old photo of the place or, if a photo wasn't available, a crinkled old memory, and would regale Richard with the bullet points of his hard-luck past, all of which added up to the simple phrase: *I had to earn it, Richard.* It was true, Richard knew. His father had earned enough to even own his past.

Still, when Richard opened his front door that morning and a messenger handed him his father's remains, housed handsomely inside a platinum urn that was likely more valuable than anything Richard had ever owned or filched, he couldn't help but notice how light the contents were. At most, his father weighed five pounds. It was a wonder to Richard that a man of his father's cosmic weight could be cooked down to this final compound.

He brought the urn over to his coffee table and set it down next to a stack of magazines and newspapers that all bore notices of his father's passing. The owner of the

Yankees called Deuce "a true pioneer" while the commissioner of baseball mentioned a legacy of "hard bargaining" and the owner of the A's remembered how Deuce "always found the loophole and was as driven on the golf course as he was in the front office." Richard's childhood hero, the former Mariner First Baseman Alvin Bradley, said that Deuce was "the first person to show faith in my abilities."

When Richard read these plaudits, the first thought that occurred to him was that it was like reading an algebraic equation where the answer is given but the path to the answer remains mysterious. He'd seen the Yankees' owner actually slap his father. The commissioner of baseball, back when he still owned the Brewers, once left a message with an eleven-year-old Richard that started, "Tell your asshole of a father that I demand a call back." He was also fairly certain that the owner of the A's had slept with his mother simply out of revenge. Alvin Bradley? Well, good old Alvin had been one of Richard's best clients in the late '90s, back when he was moving crank in and out of Phoenix, and had told him on more than one occasion that it was Richard's father who got him hooked on uppers back in the day.

Of course Deuce was also lauded for his philanthropy, particularly for breast cancer awareness (which had claimed Richard's mother) and his role in helping to open up shipping lines to China, and his sentient move into the coffee business back when people were still paying fifty cents for a refillable cup.

The weird thing was, prior to receiving the will, Richard hadn't really felt much of anything about his father's passing other than a troubling sense of relief. He'd tried to cry a little bit when the news first hit. He was watching SportsCenter in bed, where he'd been spending much of his days and nights since his sister passed, and the anchors did their grave faces and muted tones bit before flashing a photo of Deuce with the dates of his life typed neatly beneath his chin. The first thing he thought was, *That's no good.* And then he thought, *I should cry.* And then he tried to do just that, but nothing came. He pictured his sister in her casket—something he didn't actually see as her husband called him and told him to stay away—and that brought the tears, but once he tried to transfer them to his father . . . nothing.

But now, with his father resting in peace on his bong-water stained coffee table, he couldn't shake the sense that he sort of wanted to crawl into the urn with him, or at least grab a handful of his ashes tight between his hands, to let his father know that he wasn't alone. Why else would he have wanted his ashes spread out over a domed baseball diamond—particularly one with artificial surface, which meant he was likely to be vacuumed up or sucked into the dome's ventilation system and spit back out into downtown Seattle—unless he was afraid of being alone?

The first time Richard was arrested, when he was nineteen, his father actually came down to the Manhattan Beach jail to bail him out, but not before asking the cop on duty at the boutique cop shop to show him his son's cell. Deuce stood there for a good ten minutes just staring at his son and the eight by eight slab of concrete Richard was drying out in. Richard remembered well the pained look on his father's face, as if he were the one who'd spent the night trying to sleep on the piss-smelling institutional mat.

"You get used to this," Deuce said. "You remember this place. You remember how small and lonely it is, and then, next time you feel like shaming me, maybe you'll opt to take another route."

"You think I wanted to be here?" Richard said. "This wasn't my choice, Dad. You put me in this position."

"That's your excuse?" Deuce said. "That it wasn't your *choice*? You've decided to live your life blaming others, Richard; that's your big *choice*. If this is your path, then I'm not afraid to say that you won't be missed."

A cop came up then, roused by Deuce's rising tenor no doubt, and unlocked Richard's cell. By the time Richard had collected his personal effects—a wallet on a chain, Doc Martens, and a Swiss Army knife he'd received for his fifteenth birthday all sealed nicely in a plastic bag—his father was long gone.

And yet, after all these years, after all the fighting, after trying to forget his father, after being arrested at least thirty more times, each arrest earning a bullet point on the sports wire, here Richard was, face-to-face with his father, and he still had nothing to offer, not even a decent burial.

Walking through the Forest Lawn Cemetery on Saturday, his father's urn tucked under his arm in an insulated Trader Joe's shopping bag along with the will, Richard couldn't help but notice how many of the people he saw actually appeared fairly happy. Of course there were a share of people crowded in the distance around mounds of fresh dirt who were unquestionably sad, but the people Richard encountered as he worked his way through the maze of gravestones in search of his sister's seemed to be uniformly in good spirits. Richard counted at least a half dozen family picnics, several bounding dogs, and at least one full-scale birthday for a young child, balloons and clown included.

So Richard wasn't terribly surprised when he encountered three older Mexican men sitting in folding chairs around the gravestone just adjacent to Amy's. They had a small radio that was playing Tejano music at a respectful level, a cooler filled with bottles of beer, soda, and sandwiches, and an arthritic-looking golden retriever that managed to look quite at home lying across the grave. Richard tried not to make eye contact with anyone, not even the dog, but as he passed, one of the men waved at him and smiled, so Richard sputtered out a quick, "How you doing?" hoping the man would just nod in response.

"Blessed," the man said.

"Happy to hear it," Richard said. He tried to keep walking, but the man—he couldn't have been less than seventy, and years in the sun had turned his flesh ruddy and thick—stood up and motioned Richard over to the cooler.

"You like a beer? We have plenty."

"No thanks," Richard said, though he dearly did. The other men were just as old, maybe a year or two separated each of them. Richard looked at the gravestone and saw that it read: *Manuela Rios, Devoted Mother, Sister, Wife. 1910–1972. Now and Forever In God's Hands.* Thirty-five years Manuela Rios had been dead and still there were people who cared enough to throw a little fiesta for her. Richard doubted anyone would bother to do likewise for him, at least not those who knew him now. When he looked back up, all three men—and the dog—were staring at him. "I'm sorry for your loss," he mumbled, because he couldn't figure out what to say, having never attended a picnic on top of a corpse, but the three men didn't seem to hear him or, if they did, didn't bother to react. Of course not, he thought, it's been thirty-five years! It's not a loss anymore, it's a fucking fact. He wasn't sure precisely when loss stopped being simple sorrow and turned into a condition of your existence, but he was beginning to suspect that it was something like an undertow and that he wouldn't be aware of it until he was far off to sea with no way of getting back to shore.

The man motioned toward the elaborate marble headstone only a few feet away. "You here for Amy Charsten?" the man asked.

It was so weird hearing Amy's name come from this man's mouth, the way her entire life had ended up as two words uttered by a stranger in a cemetery. Amy was proud of her name, proud that she was the only woman alive who had it, proud that she'd found a man who didn't care that she'd decided to keep it when she married, and now that was all that was left of her. Whatever was underground wasn't his twin sister, Richard knew, because he was still alive and he was part of her, was her, could have been her.

"She was my twin sister," Richard said. "I haven't made it out here before, but I felt like it was time."

"Yeah," the man said. "Well, her husband say, you know, if I see you here call him and he'll call the cops. He even gave me a photo." The man reached into his back pocket, pulled out his wallet, and from there retrieved a folded picture and handed it to Richard. It was actually a photo of Amy and Richard sitting together on the swing Amy had on her back porch, except that Amy had been dutifully sliced out of the frame. Or, more like it, Richard had been sliced out. Richard remembered precisely when it was taken: Thanksgiving, 1999. He'd just gotten out of jail the day before, and Amy had graciously taken him into her home in the gated compound in Calabasas. The next day,

Amy presented him with the keys to his apartment and, she said, "a new lease on life." They'd both laughed at the silly pun, and for a few moments they'd just been brother and sister again. It was one of those memories he'd latched onto after her death, looking for some deeper resonance.

"That's me," Richard said and attempted to hand the photo back.

"No, no," the man said. "You keep it. We're here every week, you know, just being with our mother, and we don't see Amy's husband but twice since the funeral, so we say, you know, maybe we'll call the cops on him for not being here more, that's what we should do."

Richard just nodded. When all of this will business was settled, he'd get in contact with Jeff, his brother-in-law, and just tell him how it was all a mistake, one of a series of terrible mistakes, one that ended up being the culmination of all the worst decisions of his life. He'd do that. In fact, he decided, he'd give Jeff half of everything. Maybe two-thirds. Maybe he'd give him 90 percent. How much money did he actually need? Not $250 million, certainly. Not even $25 million. He might give 99 percent to Jeff, just take the yacht and some scratch for food and beer. And then what? A life of leisure? Yes. Yes. He'd earned that. *Hadn't* he earned that? Hadn't he suffered enough to live out the next fifty years in relative comfort? Wasn't it his time?

But before he could even dwell on that possibility, Richard found himself slumped over and sobbing, the Mexican man patting him gently on the back, telling him it would all be okay, that it gets better, that it can suffocate you unless you handle it, but Richard wasn't even sure who he was crying for. What was he doing here? Why had he bothered to bring his father's ashes? What did he think he'd accomplish? That he'd place Deuce's ashes next to Amy's grave, he'd spread out the will, and the three of them would just hash it out until someone came up with a way for Richard to claim his inheritance? He would have been better off bringing in Tarot cards and a fucking shaman.

It was all out in front of him, though Richard couldn't accurately pinpoint what "it" was. He thought it might be something about getting what was deserved, something he'd earned, something he'd value for the rest of his life: the opportunity to *try* on a new skin, a new life, push forward into the sunset of existence with an idea that there was equity in all of the failure. For nearly two decades he'd believed that his father had cursed him that first day in the cell in Manhattan Beach—a cell he'd recall as the nicest one he'd had the pleasure of drying out in—but now things were starting to filter out into clearer focus. *You won't be missed.* It wasn't a curse, Richard understood now, it was a premonition. There was always a loophole.

Eventually, the Mexican men must have determined that Richard needed to be alone with his sobbing, because they quietly packed up their beer and folding chairs and left him alone in the damp grass at the base of Amy's grave, where he sat for a long time reading through Deuce's will, slowly realizing that the loophole was right where it should be.

Richard often thought of his mistakes as being like falling into and out of love. When you were deep in with someone new, figuring out what felt right and shit, everything was electric.

It's all sex in public places, boozy nights, and secret-telling. But actually being in love, sustaining love, is a fucking bear. It's taxes and phone bills and excuses and lies and degradation and where do you end up? Regretting everything, trying to piece together how you could have ever made such a foolish decision as to whom to love and trust. At some point—and Richard felt he'd crossed a precipice in this regard—you decide you do not want to be defined by your worst mistakes.

The unfortunate thing, Richard knew now, standing shirtless in the backyard of Deuce's childhood home in Sarasota, spreading red clay across a swatch of AstroTurf, was that it took him thirty-five years plus ten long days and now, well, a single night to figure out how to break the cycle without falling off the bike all together. What was deserved ultimately was what one already had. *Trying* had only reinforced in Richard the sense that he could steal identities and apply them to himself any old time he pleased without any regard for karmic ramifications or simple, unmitigated guilt.

Richard didn't love his father, was content that he probably never would, but he did love his twin sister, Amy. As he shoveled the last bit of clay into place and then tamped it down with the back of the spade, he tried to think of how it was for them when they were kids, how when they were little they looked so much alike that strangers always thought Amy was a boy, too. He remembered small things that weren't significant but had somehow hardwired into his brain. Eating Pronto Pups and saltwater taffy together in Seaside, Oregon, and giggling about . . . what was it? Some joke they used to tell each other, he recalled that, something about corn dogs and taffy that they'd turned into a riddle of some kind. Anointing each other charter members of the Creepy Crawly Club for their stealth ability to break into and out of the kitchen after bedtime. The way Richard used to sneak into Amy's room at night when he couldn't sleep and would lie on the floor beside her bed and replicate her breathing rhythm until he, too, fell asleep.

Richard was already aware that he'd begun to forget aspects of his sister. Sometimes he would stare at himself in the mirror and try to imagine that he was his sister, that he was the one who'd died, and what would she be feeling? They were the same person, cut from the same piece of whole cloth, and yet they'd been separated over the years by inertia. She always in motion, he always at rest. And now, inexplicably, it had flipped. All that was left of his sister was himself, and Richard felt a debt to that.

Amy's last words for him hadn't felt like the stuff of epiphany, but he realized now, as he walked down the first base line he'd painted in painstaking detail on Major League quality AstroTurf, that he'd count them as the first sign of a newfound hope. *Stop fucking up*. He would do that. He would. He *will*, he thinks. He *will*.

Richard conceded, however, that Amy might have approved of this last bit of criminal activity—breaking into and vandalizing a home he didn't own and never would—since the result aimed for a greater good, if only briefly. He even purchased the supplies himself, did all the measuring, made sure the dimensions matched exactly, and even went beyond what was probably strictly needed to meet the conditions of the will so that, if his father chose to haunt this space, he could sprint from home, down to first, and make the turn toward second into perpetuity.

It was nearly midnight when Richard finally looked at his watch, which meant that Deuce's law office was probably long closed and all the Calvin Woodses of the world were already at home living their separate lives, and it wouldn't be until tomorrow that they realized Richard Charsten III had pissed away an empire.

Richard went out to his rental car and retrieved Deuce's ashes and a change of clothes from a duffle bag in the trunk. He set Deuce down on home plate while he silently changed into a suit and tie, along with a pair of reasonable dress shoes he'd purchased at Target before flying to Sarasota. When he was dressed, Richard wet a black pocket comb with his tongue and managed to get his hair into the semblance of a part. He wasn't sure if he should say something while he spread his father's ashes down the first base line of the Seattle Kingdome, or if he should remain in solemn silence, but he figured, if appropriate, words would come, or thoughts would come, and he would make them last.

# Other Resort Cities

**T**hree days after she gets back from Russia with Natalya, her adopted daughter, Tania knows that she's made a mistake. It's ten in the morning and they're walking through the new New York, New York Casino, Tania pointing out how the faux Statue of Liberty out front is *actually* half the scale of the real statue, how when Tania's ancestral family first came to America, they *actually* came right past the Statue of Liberty, too. How the casino floor is *actually* a replica of Central Park, right down to the trees and the piped-in bird noises.

Seventy-two hours into their new life together and Tania has already run out of conversation topics, is now making things up as she goes along, this word "actually" creeping back into her vocabulary for the first time since the year she spent lying to everyone. How old was she then? Sixteen or seventeen, though she could have been fifteen or eighteen. It may have been longer than a year. It may have *actually* been a period. Back then, she lied because she had nothing else to say, nothing interesting whatsoever, and frequently told stories to her friends about *actually* spending a year in England when she was ten, or how her real father was *actually* Walter Cronkite, because it was better than simply being someone's second daughter.

But now here it is, the last Saturday in March 1997, and she is thirty-five years old and telling lies to her own child only to avoid the realization that this whole adoption, the entire process of bringing Natalya to the States, must have been folly on her part.

"Are you hungry?"

"Some," Natalya says. It's one of about fifty English words Tania has grown tired of hearing since first meeting Natalya in Russia last month. Before actually adopting Natalya, after having only seen her photo and reading her letters (which, she knows now, Natalya never actually wrote, but were likely form letters with blanks for specific U.S. cities and American names), Tania envisioned that Natalya, though already twelve, would have an infantlike personality filled with abject need and wonder, such that every moment would be like a revelation to the girl. Tania would keep a scrapbook with pictures of "Natalya's first Big Mac" and "Natalya's bicycle," and eventually it would just say "Nat's" this and "Nat's" that as things got more personal.

Instead she discovered this . . . girl, this half-woman, who wanted nothing but to be left alone, who had spent most every night on the Internet chatting with friends in Russia or crying, and who never directly addressed Tania at all. But Tania isn't even sure what she'd like Natalya to call her. The word "mom" has so many connotations she's simply not comfortable with, plus there's the issue that Natalya still remembers her own mother, who, if the people at the orphanage in Russia are to be believed, was a scientist. The orphanage told Tania that both of Natalya's parents were scientists who died in a car accident en route to a very prestigious conference. At the time, this fact gave Tania a sense of true ebullience: *My daughter might be a scientist, too!*

Now, though, she doubts any of it might be true. Scientists, particularly ones who attended prestigious conferences, probably had extended families, probably wouldn't have left Natalya in an orphanage in Tula for nine years while she waited to be adopted by an American.

"We should get out of this casino," Tania says. "Have you ever had a taco?"

"Some," Natalya says.

"I didn't know there were Mexicans in Russia," Tania says, but Natalya doesn't respond. She's learned already that Natalya has no ear for sarcasm yet, that her limited sum of English is based mostly on basic human services like eating, sleeping, and going to the bathroom, her most complex sentence to date being the one she uttered as their plane circled Las Vegas three nights ago: *Why so many lights?* she asked. "It's so people can see that they're having a good time," Tania told her, but that didn't seem to satisfy Natalya. She spread her fingers out across the window, blocking out entire swatches of the city, so that all that was visible were the Red Rock Mountains and the muted lights of the city's suburban sprawl. "Better," she said.

Every ten minutes, another plane swoops over the Taco Bell on Maryland Parkway either en route to or just taking off from McCarron Airport. Outside, where Tania and Natalya are sitting eating their tacos in silence, Tania watches how Natalya follows the path of each plane with her eyes. Her expression remains fairly placid, but Tania thinks the girl shows a bit more sadness for each plane that lands, though she recognizes immediately how stupid that is. The girl is sad about everything. It's impossible she's now assigned metaphors for her sadness, at least not ones as absurd as Southwest planes, particularly since one of those planes will deliver Tania's own parents within the hour. "We can't wait to meet our granddaughter," Joan, Tania's mother, said on the phone the day previous. "We're bringing all the old scrapbooks so she can see pictures of you when you were a little girl. Won't she get a kick out of that?"

"I don't think that's a great idea," Tania said. "Everything is already moving so fast for her."

"They're just pictures," Joan said. "Don't you think she'll want to see what her mother was like when she was twelve? I remember when you came home from spending the summer with your Nana and couldn't wait to tell me about seeing pictures of me in bobby socks and a poodle skirt."

"I'm not her mother," Tania said.

"You have to be," Joan said.

The problem for Tania is not the concept that she's now Natalya's mother, but rather the execution. Natalya is nothing like her, there's no seed of similarity to grasp yet that binds her to Natalya apart from the curve of the girl's upper lip. It was the first thing Tania noticed when the orphanage in Russia sent her those first photos a year ago. The photos were several years old and showed Natalya posed around a metal jungle gym. In each, Natalya had either a piece of candy or an ice cream cone in her hand and was dressed in an adorable red velvet outfit. Her face was so alive in those photos, her smile nothing short of infectious, and her lip, the way it moved into a soft point when she was particularly happy in those shots. How many people had Tania ever made *that* happy, ever? To be able to give this child the chance to make that face . . . it overwhelmed Tania, to the point that she printed out those photos and showed them to the other cocktail girls at the Mirage, told them, "This is my daughter," and when they asked if she lived with an ex or something, Tania just nodded. Something. Certainly something.

But the face in those early pictures is lost now beneath too much makeup—she'd have to make Natalya wash her face before the parents landed—and a scowl so persistent that Tania has begun to think that perhaps there was a clerical mistake somewhere in the process and that she was allowed to adopt the wrong child. Somewhere in Tula, Russia, is a happy girl with the same cute little lip Natalya has, and she's waiting patiently for Tania to return and rectify the situation.

Tania had failed to consider that the years between when those first photos were taken and now would have aged Natalya. She knew it rationally, of course; knew that adopting a twelve-year-old girl came with its own specific set of problems. But Tania couldn't stand the idea of being one of those forty-year-old women still toting around an infant like an accessory. She imagined Natalya as an instant friend, as well as someone she could actually talk to, but also as a child who would need her. The first time she actually saw Natalya in Tula, however, she realized how juvenile her thinking had been: Natalya was sitting at a picnic table not far from the jungle gym in the old photos, reading aloud from a picture book to three small boys, and even from her vantage point fifty yards away, Tania could tell that Natalya had presence, personality, a life.

"Are you happy?" Tania asks.

Natalya cocks her head, as if to make sure she's heard correctly, but doesn't answer right away. Tania isn't sure how much English Natalya actually knows. The people at the orphanage said she was "75 percent fluent," which Tania thought was fairly remarkable in light of how many people she knew in Las Vegas who were probably closer to 50 percent and held management positions at the hotel. What she's learned in the month they've spent together—first during the bureaucratic morass of court hearings and meetings in Russia, where legally she was only allowed to spend fifteen unsupervised minutes each day with Natalya, and now as they've walked this odd alien tightrope in Tania's Summerlin townhouse—is that Natalya can read well enough but that she's selective in what she can say or understand of spoken English. Tania's sister tells her that's normal for a twelve-year-old born in America, too, which would be funny to Tania if it was her own flesh that ignored her. But this child, this child who cost her nearly all of the $50,000 she won on a single hand of Caribbean Stud on the same night they closed the Sands, wasn't really hers at all.

"I am not," Natalya says.

"Can you be?"

Natalya fingers her cup of Sprite and looks away from Tania, out toward the street, which has suddenly filled with college students exiting UNLV. It's noon, though with the persistent case of jet lag she has, it feels much later, but also somehow slower to Tania. She imagines Natalya must feel something entirely different, though, and for the first time since they arrived back in Las Vegas, Tania begins to feel sorry for Natalya. For her dead parents, for this woman who has shown up in her life and brought her to America, forced her to eat tacos, made her answer questions about how she feels, when the woman herself has only the vaguest sense of her own emotions.

"One day, maybe," Natalya says. "This place is so different. Not like home."

"I'm going to work on that," Tania says, though the truth is that she has no idea how she'll change anything. She's been in school for the last six months trying to become a dental hygienist, to give herself—and her daughter—a chance at a life outside Las Vegas, but has failed chemistry twice in that span. If she couldn't master an even rudimentary understanding of the composition, structure, and properties of matter, how could she claim to know anything? "I want to be a good parent to you, Natalya. I've never been one before, so this is going to take some doing." Another plane roars overhead and Tania checks her watch. Her parents are due to land in another thirty minutes. "You don't have to answer this, and maybe you don't know, but I wonder what really happened to your parents?"

Natalya shrugs. "Dead," she says. "I don't know."

"Do you want to?"

"When I go back when I'm older," Natalya says.

Of course she'll go back. Tania had already entertained the idea of one day having a home in Tula, too, so that Natalya wouldn't grow up thinking she was some kind of refugee, so that she knew she hadn't escaped, that she was still tethered to her past, even if her future, if the people who really loved her (and this was when Tania was sure she already loved Natalya, before this sense of emotional burden began its slow descent), now lived in America.

On her third day in Tula, she'd rented a car and just drove, not bothering to consult the map of tourist locales—she'd never read any Tolstoy, so visiting his home didn't seem necessary, and she wasn't very excited about the prospect of visiting the Museum of Russian Weapons, either—hoping instead to stumble into neighborhoods, the kind perhaps Natalya had lived in as a toddler and where they might live together, or at least visit.

She discovered a neighborhood just adjacent to the local university, only a few miles west of the twisting Upa River. It was the mid-morning—a time she rarely saw in Las Vegas, since her shift at the Mirage typically ran 9:00 PM to 6:00 AM, which meant she usually was heading to bed just as normal people were waking up—so the streets were alive with college students, but also with people who just looked like regular humans, people like her who served the people who bothered to go to school. There was a main drag of coffee shops and stores interspersed with one-story houses with flat roofs, but on large slats of green land. She was surprised by the lack of fences surrounding the homes here, but also by the lack of trash on the street. *Yes,* she thought, *we could live in this place. I could learn the language. I could go to school. We could drink coffee on the street and read Tolstoy together.*

When she returned to the orphanage and told Leda, the administrator she dealt with most closely, that she'd found the most perfect neighborhood for them to one day return to, Leda brushed her off quickly. "Very polluted there from Chernobyl," she said. "Most of Tula is."

"Then how do people live here?"

"You have to live somewhere."

That was true enough, Tania knew. She'd lived in Spokane, Reno, and Las Vegas in her life, each place as unremarkable as the previous, but the thing that always amazed her, even when she simply went out of town for a few days, like when she went on a cruise to Mexico with a few girlfriends back when she worked at the Cal-Neva, was how much she missed her *spaces*, how comforting it was to know she could never get lost in these resort cities other people visited.

And now this child. This new life. Somehow she'd figured out the only way to muddle her existence beyond recognition. I should tell her I'm sorry, Tania thinks. That this was all very selfish of me. That I can return her.

"Do you remember your parents?" Tania asks. All Tania knows for sure about Natalya's parents is their medical history, which includes a history of cancer and heart disease on both sides of the family. "Nobody dies from being healthy," Leda, the administrator, told her. "Everybody dies from something awful."

"My father had a beard." Natalya's watching the planes again, and Tania wonders if in ten years she'll be as scantily recalled. "And my mother was pretty," Natalya says. "Like you."

No one chooses to cocktail, Tania thinks. She and her family— her parents, Stu and Joan, and Natalya—are waiting for a table at Odessa, the one Russian restaurant in all of Las Vegas. It's in a strip mall off of Paradise, a few blocks south of Flamingo. Tania has strenuously avoided the place over the years, since it was one of those restaurants in town everyone said was mob owned, like the Venetian on Sahara and Piero's over by the convention center. But now she sees that it's filled with families, that the waiters are all older men with mustaches wearing black pants and spotless white shirts. The cocktail girls hovering around the people playing video poker in the bar, however, look the same as everywhere: low-cut tops, hair sprayed and teased, shoes no woman would ever consent to walk in on her own. One of the girls looks familiar, though Tania can't quite place her, thinks maybe she worked at the Excalibur with her when she first got to town, or maybe she picked up a few shifts at the Mirage, or . . . well, it didn't matter. She wasn't going to say hello anyway. Wherever they knew each other from, that time was over, and now the girl was working in a strip mall.

Since landing three hours ago, Tania's mother has been lecturing Natalya on American history, telling her interesting tidbits about the League of Nations and Woodrow Wilson, and now, in the restaurant, has worked all the way up to the Hoover Dam, but Tania's not taking part, instead she's watching the restaurant, watching the people serving, thinking about how difficult it is to know who you're going to be when you're just a kid. What did she want to do with her life? She never decided, though she knows now it wasn't cocktailing. That's the job you end up with when you've made no decisions at all; or at least none that matter. And then one day that's just who you are.

Maybe, you wait long enough, people just end up making decisions for you without your knowledge, and then you wake up and you're fifty, hustling tips over Chicken Kiev.

"Isn't this place great?" Joan asks. She's sitting between Tania and Natalya and keeps grabbing at both of their wrists. It's something Tania remembers she used to do in church whenever there was something interesting happening and Joan wanted to get Tania and her sister Justine's attention. It was Joan's idea to come here in the first place—she read about it in a tourist guide to Las Vegas—and they weren't five minutes out of the airport before she was telling Tania how great it would be to have authentic Russian food for dinner, as if she'd ever had inauthentic Russian food in the past. Now, no one knows what to talk about, and the wrist-grabbing feels like a nervous tic. "Is this what home is like?" Joan says to Natalya.

"Some," Natalya says and then forces out a smile. It's the first time Tania has seen the girl smile in days, and she can't help but feel jealous that her own mother can get Natalya to show something, anything, and here she can't even get the girl to look her in the eye most of the time.

"I think you're just going to love it here," Joan says.

Stu, Tania's father, paces in front of them. For forty years he sold restaurant equipment and now, two years into his retirement, Tania can't imagine how he ever closed any deals. He always looks vaguely displeased in restaurants, as if he can't quite figure out how, after all the time he spent working in restaurants, he's still expected to *eat* in them, too.

"Dad," Tania says, "sit. You're making me nervous."

"No," he says. "No. I'm trying to see what they're cleaning with back there. From the sound of it, I'd bet they've got a Hobart, and not one that is functioning properly. Wash cycle sounds corrupted. We're about fifteen minutes from food poisoning, if you want my opinion."

When Tania graduated high school and moved first to Reno, the idea was that she'd go to community college there for two years, establish residency, and then try to get into the hotel management program at UNLV in Las Vegas, all of which was her father's idea. He told her there would always be hotels, that people always needed to stay somewhere. Restaurants, he told her, were a luxury people could do without, but everyone needed to sleep. But then she started cocktailing at the Cal-Neva, started making what to her was real money, and eventually just stopped attending class at all. It felt, at the time, like there was plenty more to do in life than get an education, more to life than thinking about where people stayed, but now, watching her father pace, his life boiled down to his ability to parse the sounds of dishwashers, watching the cocktail girl as she casually flirts with the locals around the bar, she thinks that her own hubris has brought her to this point in life. Opting to do nothing. She'd failed to recognize how the weight of finally making a decision could be so paralyzing.

She used to tell people she was saving money to open a dog grooming business—she even had a name picked out: Groomingdales—though the fact was that she didn't have any idea how to accomplish that, didn't even know if she'd need a license or if she could just get a pair of clippers and a storefront or what. And really, since her dog died last year, just a day before she started looking into adoption options in Russia, the desire to be around animals of any kind was just too depressing to consider.

But it was silly, anyway. She never had any money saved, apart from what she won at Caribbean Stud, and that hadn't even felt like her money.

"Honey," Tania's mother says to her, "you should ask the manager if they have any job openings here for hostesses.

Wouldn't that be perfect for Natalya?" She turns to Natalya and takes her wrist again. "Wouldn't that be nice, sweetheart? Earn a little pocket money?" When Natalya doesn't answer, Joan looks back at Tania expectantly, as if this is the solution to a great many unknown problems. "Wouldn't it?"

"She's twelve," Tania says.

"In a few years then," Joan says.

"I don't want her working in a restaurant or a bar or anywhere like this," Tania says.

"It would just be something to do after school," Joan says. "You're going to need extra money, Tania."

"I'll start gambling again," Tania says. "Besides, they say the Russian mafia owns the restaurant."

"That's just silly," Joan says. "If you won't ask, I will. She could maybe meet some people from her country, too."

"I want to show you something," Tania says and pulls out a little change purse filled with business cards from her wallet and dumps the contents on her mother's lap. There are at least a hundred cards, engraved, embossed, phone numbers and room numbers and email addresses scratched onto the back of each. Tania picks a few up and waves them in front of her mother's face. "Every night, I get maybe five or six of these. You know what they want, Mom? They aren't looking to make business deals, okay? They aren't looking to make friends, okay? My daughter is not going to work in a place like this. Ever."

Tania feels as if she might cry, as if she might just let it all go right here in the middle of pleasant Russian families having dinner, as if she might stand up and start screaming, but then Natalya reaches over and takes all of the spilled business cards from Joan's lap and hands them to a passing busboy, who is actually a middle-aged Mexican, and says, "Please. To garbage."

Later that evening, after Natalya goes to sleep, Tania sits up with her parents in her small living room. Her parents have a room down the street at Arizona Charlie's, a local's casino Tania's father likes because of the pancake buffet breakfast and because he once won a satin jacket there during a blackjack tournament, but neither of them seems to be in a hurry to leave.

There are photo albums scattered across the floor, a half eaten bowl of microwave popcorn in her mother's lap. A series of photos from the night of her senior prom are still stacked on the coffee table. What does she remember about that night? Getting high, mostly. Having sex with her date—a boy named Devin—in the bathroom of the Ramada Inn, the music from the dance throbbing through the wall, Devin's breath hot on her face, her hair catching in his watchband. But mostly, mostly, she remembers wondering when it would end. When she could go home, forget these people, get on with her life. Even then, at eighteen, things seemed unsatisfying to her, as if the next day would always be the best one.

"She seems very intelligent," Stu says. At sixty-seven, and two years removed from his own real life, Tania's father now has a doughy quality to his skin and has become obsessive about odd things: the price of gas, the amount of advertising in baseball stadiums, other peoples' teeth. As a child, Tania was afraid of her father. That's not to say she felt threatened by him, only that there was a feature to his existence in her life that boiled her stomach. So maybe it wasn't fear. Maybe it was just anxiety. And then it occurs to her that it was *his* anxiety she was feeling, that she was afraid of him because he was afraid of . . . *something*.

"Her parents were scientists," Tania says.

"Is that so?" her mother says. She's barely spoken to Tania since the outburst at the restaurant, but that's fine.

"Actually," Tania says, "they were both very involved in Russia's nuclear program."

Tania's father nods his head at this, and she can see his mind filling with questions, new obsessions forming. She knows her father still considers Russia the enemy, even though the Cold War has been over for nearly a decade, and even he must know that Natalya is just a child and not some kind of sleeper agent, but she's sure he still has real concerns. Maybe that's why she's so vibrantly recalling this now. It wasn't that he brought fear into the house with him, but that he was always so circumspect, that whenever he'd watch the news or read the *Spokesman-Review* he'd start to mutter about how the whole world was made up of charlatans, that you couldn't trust anything you saw. Everything deserved investigation.

This is a period of her life that Tania associates with her mother's odd descent into religion, a time her father feels largely absent from in her memory, since he didn't actually attend church with them. Not the Wednesday night Bible study and coffee klatch the church called Supreme Bean (which, upon retrospect, strikes Tania as surprisingly clever), nor the regular Sunday service. Though since they only had one car, a blue Ford Fairmont, he'd drive them to the church both days and then he'd just sit outside smoking. Sometimes he'd bring one of those dime-store men's adventure novels with him—*The Exterminator* or *The Destroyer* or, occasionally, a thick Robert Ludlum novel that he never seemed to finish—but usually he just sat and waited.

Once back at home, Tania's mother sat at the kitchen table and drank Sanka while she read the Bible, her lips moving over every word. She'd periodically jot a note down onto a steno pad, though Tania can't remember ever seeing her mother read back over those notes. Tania usually sat on the front lawn and watched Justine practice twirling the baton, though she doesn't know what Justine was practicing for, since she never competed, never became a member of the cheer or dance squads, while her father raked leaves, even if there weren't any leaves on the ground. On rainy days, her father would rake the avocado-colored shag carpet in their living room. She can see him standing there in the living room, a cigarette in his teeth, pulling the rake from one corner of the room to the other, making sure not to cross the lines he'd already put into the carpet.

She can't imagine how she'd forgotten this image of her father for so long, but now it's all she can envision when she looks at him sitting on her sofa, his purple-veined hands reaching into the bowl of popcorn. How old is he in this memory? Maybe forty, forty-five. Not much older than she is now, but living an entirely different life. He had two children, a wife, a job selling restaurant supplies that he'd have until the day he stopped working, a Craftsman in a decent neighborhood in Spokane, a fishing trip every June to Loon Lake. He must have wanted something more, though Tania can't imagine what. Tania doesn't know her father, really (and can't say she knows her mother, either), but she wonders if he misses the fear, the rage, the longing, or if somehow a satin jacket and a pancake buffet are enough to satiate him.

"Aren't you surprised by how nice Natalya's teeth are?" her father says. "I just assumed they'd be in really poor shape."

Tania wakes up to the sound of Natalya blow-drying her hair. It is nine in the morning on Sunday, and Tania promised Natalya that they could go to the Stratosphere today to ride the rollercoaster atop the casino's hundred-story tower. Tomorrow, she'll be back at work and Natalya will start her first day of school, so this is their last free day before real life starts, or at least that's how Tania thinks of it. She's not sure what to make of real life anymore, not sure she knows how to conduct herself, except that she realizes she needs to change her shift at the hotel, or else Natalya will be home all night by herself. Last night her mother offered to move in for a couple of weeks if Tania thought it would help ease Natalya into her routine, but Tania told her no, that she'd be fine, but the reality was that she didn't want her mother to see how unprepared she really was, that she hadn't even thought about such a simple task as getting her shift moved.

She pulls herself out of bed and looks outside, makes sure her car is still parked under the metal awning across the way. She lives in a townhouse in Summerlin, which is just a fancy way of saying that she lives in an apartment that happens to have a connected one-car garage beneath it, one she's filled with so much of her crap that she doesn't have room to park her Explorer. Her neighbors are mostly working girls— strippers, other cocktail waitresses like herself, blackjack and roulette dealers—and young families. It's a safe neighborhood and the complex is gated, but even still, she's aware of how vulnerable she is living alone, and now, living with Natalya. Her ex-boyfriend, Clive, who worked the door at a strip club called Little Darlings, used to tell her stories about girls who got followed home after work and were robbed and then either raped or killed or both, but because they were just dancers, and usually didn't even really live in Las Vegas, just kept a place for the weekends they danced in town, no one bothered to check on them for days or weeks and then, well, then it didn't matter who they were anymore. They were just dead strippers from that point forward.

Long ago she'd convinced herself that Clive's stories were just myths, though of course anything was possible in Las Vegas. Things would be different now, anyway. She wouldn't date guys like Clive, people who were all about bringing negativity in the absence of anything valuable. Her sister, Justine, was always saying how great it was that Tania had such a wide market of available men to date in Las Vegas, particularly single guys with money, but the truth was that no one who spent much time visiting Las Vegas was the kind of guy who would be right to help her raise Natalya. Circumstances had changed, and now here she was not even sure a person like herself was capable of the job.

She hadn't even really been with a guy since hitting the royal. She'd done a stupid thing that night and left her job at the Mirage with a customer, a Persian guy named Pejman who said he was a doctor from Seattle, but was probably just another dumb ass from LA with a little money in his pocket for the weekend, which, honestly, didn't bother her, really.

He had some coke, a gold Amex, and wanted to party. He tipped her over a grand that night, slipping her bills every ten minutes while he rolled craps, convinced she was his luck. And maybe she was, because she put $500 of his tips on that Stud game, flopped a royal, and found herself $50,000 richer.

The thing was, she ended up fucking that guy in his room at the Frontier (which should have been her first clue he wasn't a doctor), and now, a year later, all she can remember about him is that he wore these absurd black and white saddle shoes, like he was ten and on his way to the sandbox. Would that be the story she eventually told Natalya about how she came to have enough money to afford her adoption? That she fucked a guy in saddle shoes who tipped her a grand that she turned around on a fucking table game?

Tania hears the blow-dryer click off, and the townhouse fills with the sound of Natalya singing to herself in Russian. The melody sounds familiar, though Tania can't quite place it—she thinks it might be an old Michael Jackson song, maybe Prince, something she hears over the Muzak piped into the Mirage—but the words she's saying in Russian make the song sound exquisite and nuanced. Something more than just a pop song about love or dancing or partying the millennium away. Tania knows intellectually that she should learn Russian, but she hasn't done it, thinks that not knowing how to speak Russian will give Natalya a better sense of privacy, a way to escape. And anyway, if she knew the language, she'd lose the ability to appreciate the sound of Natalya singing in it.

Down on the street a Yellow Cab pulls up in front of her townhouse, and Chelsea, Tania's next-door neighbor, steps out into the sunlight. She dances over at the Olympic

Gardens, which means she's just getting home from her shift. Tania watches as Chelsea fumbles through her purse looking for cab fare. Tania can tell from one story up that Chelsea is trashed, thinks that maybe she should run downstairs to make sure Chelsea doesn't give the cabbie a stack of hundreds accidentally, see that she gets into her place okay, doesn't end up passed out on her front porch (which has happened before).

Tania considers Chelsea a good friend, though the truth is that she doesn't even know if Chelsea is her real name or just her stage name and has never bothered to ask, figuring that if she knows, she'll have to start volunteering information about herself, too. Sometimes, they go to the pool together in the afternoon before their respective shifts, and Chelsea regales her with stories from the strip club, all of which strike Tania as being tragic, in or out of context. There's the girl who sells her used underwear online, the girl whose brother is her pimp, the girl who left the club one night as a blonde with brown eyes and then came back the next day with brown hair and blue colored contacts and pretended she was a different girl entirely, even when everyone clearly recognized her, and demanded people call her by her new name.

What did Chelsea really know about Tania? Nothing, really. Tania hadn't even told her she was adopting Natalya, only that she was going to be out of town for about a month, and if she could keep an eye on her Explorer and water her plants, she'd be ever grateful. When she got home, all of her plants were dead but her car was still there, covered in bird shit, and with a thousand more miles on it than when she left. What did it mean that she wasn't surprised (or angered) in the least by this?

"Who is that?"

Tania turns and sees that Natalya has come into her bedroom and is watching the scene over her shoulder. Her long black hair is pulled away from her face and into a ponytail, her makeup, so severe yesterday, is almost nonexistent today. Tania thinks she sees the child from the photos, thinks she sees a young woman, thinks she sees someone that could have grown up to be her daughter.

"Nobody," Tania says. "No one at all."

Tania has never liked heights and yet here she is on the observation deck of the Stratosphere, nearly one hundred stories above the Las Vegas Strip, her twelve year-old adopted daughter beside her, staring out through the bowed Plexiglas window at the street below. The day has turned overcast and muggy, and from her vantage point in the sky, Tania can see heat lightning snapping between the clouds clustering to the west over Interstate 15, though the sun still cuts through the clouds intermittently. From up here the world is so tiny and unmovable to Tania; like it is under water. Everything looks wet and gray and yellow as if the clouds are bleeding the fluorescent lights off the Strip, floating between what is real and what is imaginary. Even the air seems distant and colored. Tania thinks she could jump and just float and float.

An announcement rings out over the loudspeaker that the next batch of riders for the rollercoaster should make their way to the elevator to shoot up the remaining five stories to the very top of the tower, where they will spin upside down, where they will corkscrew through the air, where no one will pay any attention that there's a woman coming to realize that the only mistake she has made was waiting so long to start this phase of her life, was being so selfish, so stupid to think that she could just pick up in the middle, that she could replace her own empty life with this other person.

Natalya is already walking toward the elevator when a strange sense of vertigo strikes Tania and she grabs at the metal railing in front of her, as if it can stop the sudden perception that she is seeing too much, that somehow the world has flipped over and she's no longer someone's daughter at all; that she's a woman, that she's responsible, that life is starting now, that everything else has been mere prelude.

"Natalya," she says, and the girl stops, turns around, looks at her. Tania would like to believe that there is some recognition in her daughter's eyes, that the girl sees in Tania the same thing that Tania feels. That she does love her. That she will never love her. That she thinks she already knows Natalya completely, because that poor girl is her, was her, could be her, wishes she was her. That she doesn't know her in the least. That she will spend her lifetime looking for Natalya's parents, dead or alive, if that's what the girl wants. Or she will never mention them again. She will never mention them again, because Natalya will not need them.

That she doesn't know if she'll ever know her enough.

Tania could let Natalya go up that elevator to the top of the Stratosphere by herself, and by the time the rollercoaster ride was up, she could be back in her Explorer and heading out of town for good, could disappear into another life. It's a thought she has had over and over again since they arrived back in Las Vegas. It's a thought she knows makes her unstable, unfit to be a parent, unlikely to give

Natalya any kind of life at all.

"Are you scared?" Natalya asks.

"Yes," Tania says.

Natalya walks back and takes Tania by the hand and pulls her along toward the elevator, pulling her past the couple in the matching Circus Circus T-shirts, past the men in tight pants with shiny silver rodeo buckles on their belts, past the teenagers with pierced eyebrows, past the old man and old woman with fanny packs and into the elevator where they stand pressed against the back wall of the car. As a child, Tania's father used to take her and her sister to Riverfront Park in downtown Spokane to ride the attractions left over from the 1974 World's Fair, but what she recalls now is that he never went on any of the rides. He'd stand outside the Tilt-a-Whirl, or the Spider, or the Bumper Cars and he'd just watch, so that whenever Tania got scared (which was often), she always knew she could find him standing there, already looking directly at her, always ready to meet her gaze. Perhaps it was out of fear. Perhaps it was out of love, even a love born out of simple duty. But it was perpetual.

The elevator doors close and Tania becomes aware of how close she is to Natalya, how she can feel her daughter's pulse through the grasp of her fingers, can smell her perfume and her shampoo and something indistinct that reminds her of being seven. And in that brief moment when the car shoots upward and the world turns buoyant, all that Tania finally perceives is the weight of her daughter's hand in her own, and she decides she will force herself to remember this moment, that she will hold it as precious, even if she's not sure now if it means anything at all.

# Rainmaker

**P**rofessor William Cooperman hated teaching in the summer. The information was always the same no matter the season, of course, but for Cooperman it was more about the students. If you were taking Introduction to Hydrology in the middle of July, that meant you'd spent the entire year avoiding it, or had failed it in the fall and only now were thinking that maybe you'd spend a few weeks getting the F off your record, maybe earn yourself a D and be done with it. That was the problem with students today. No one ever thought that understanding how water worked on the planet was vital, never even paused to consider how something as simple as sprinklers had changed the course of human development, or that it was eventually all going to turn to shit in this world and water would be a commodity you'd kill for; no compunction whatsoever.

No, he thought, sitting behind his narrow desk at the front of the lecture hall, his thirty-five students midway through the fifth pop quiz he'd proffered to them in just two weeks, these students today just didn't want to fail *water*. His students couldn't see beyond the moment, couldn't understand that the ripples they were causing would eventually be tsunamis. Didn't matter if it was water or gasoline or not caring about their bodies, kids today just didn't grasp the enormity of the predicament.

Kids. That was the other thing. Cooperman was only forty, still felt pretty much like a kid himself, like he could just as easily be sitting on the other side of the desk. He'd sit in the third row, next to Katie Williard. She seemed nice, and everyone in the class sort of gravitated around her during breaks, not only because she always had Altoids, which was true, but also to ask questions or to see if she wanted to study with them. She wasn't pretty, at least not in the classic sense, was actually sort of fat and not in that Freshman Fifteen kind of way, but rather as if she'd always battle with her weight. If she had kids, man, forget it, she'd be huge, but Cooperman thought that if she just sort of lived her life normally, didn't bother to procreate, she'd be . . . stout. He frankly liked that in a woman, if only because it told him she actually was a human being who might eat a cheeseburger every now and then.

He checked his watch. It was 2:13. Cal State Fullerton required him to hold class until precisely 2:30 each day, so that the students would get the exact amount of contact hours they needed, lest some state accreditation auditor pulling undercover duty in the class was just waiting to pounce on the college for skirting the rules. And then he had another section at 7:00, which meant his whole day was lost. Cooperman thought all of them at the college were a bunch of fucking Communists as it was, but this slavish dedication to time didn't jibe with his thoughts on higher education, which is perhaps why he was just an adjunct professor. The way Cooperman figured it, education shouldn't keep a clock. If it took five minutes to teach something, what was the use of sitting around for another hour talking about it? Especially in the summer. And on a Thursday, everyone's last day of class? It was useless, so the pop quizzes were his way of getting around that issue of talking, of actually fielding questions. Invariably someone would finish the quiz before 2:30, but the social Darwinism at play in the lecture hall essentially forced them to stay seated until a reasonable point, which was usually about 2:15.

But for some reason the students were spending more and more time on the tests, as if they were actually thinking about each question, and the result was that class was not only going the prescribed length, sometimes it went over, and that just wasn't going to work today.

Cooperman had a business meeting at the Sonic over on Lemon at 2:45 and really couldn't afford to be late. The guy he did business with, Bongo Fuentes, wasn't real big on excuses and apologies. He said he wanted to meet at 2:45 at some crap-ass drive-in fast food restaurant and you got there at 2:50? Might as well not show up at all. It occurred to Cooperman that working in academia and working in the illegal drug trade weren't all that different: people expected a certain level of punctuality, which, when you thought about it, was a really bent business model. If any two fields demanded fluidity, it was academia and drug trafficking.

The professor stood up. "Excuse me," he said, and when that didn't elicit any response, he said, "Pencils down," and then the entire room came to a full stop. It never ceased to surprise Cooperman how conditioned students were. He could have taken a shit on his desk and no one would have even looked up, but utter those two words together and it was holy sacrament. "I'm afraid I'm not feeling too well. Today, everyone gets an A on their exam. Just be sure your name is on your Blue Book when you pass it in."

There was a slight murmur in the class and immediately Cooperman knew it meant bad news. Normally, a professor says "everyone gets an A" and no one bothers to ask for any kind of explanation, but Cooperman had set a poor precedent on Monday. He'd asked everyone to turn in a two-page essay on what they perceived to be the most fascinating aspects of hydrology and then accidentally left the whole lot of them in the trunk of his rental Ford Focus, which wouldn't have been a huge problem had he not torched the rental in Mexico after it became clear he had to lose that car and lose it fast after a regrettable shooting incident. After making up a suitable lie ("I'm afraid I left all of your essays at an important conference in El Paso this past weekend."), he gave them all Bs on their papers, which caused a tribal war to break out between the Good Students, the Katie Williards of the world, and the Back Row of Fucktards, like those three frat guys whose names he intentionally didn't learn, since he was pretty sure he'd separately seen each of them purchase weed from Bongo sometime in the last year.

Predictably, Katie raised her hand.

"Yes, Ms. Williard?"

"I'm sorry, Dr. Cooperman, but I'd like to finish my exam and get the grade I earn. I think most of us feel this way."

He liked it when she called him Dr. Cooperman. And though he wasn't a PhD, he didn't bother to correct her. A little bit of respect went a long way in Cooperman's book. All these other kids? Half of them didn't even address him at all. Worse was the preponderance of adult students who'd found their way into the college after getting shit-canned from their jobs at the post office or were bounced from the police force and now found themselves in GE level courses with a bunch of kids; those students always thought they should be able to call him Will or, worse, Bill. He blamed the geology professor, James Kochel, for that particular slight, since Kochel let all of the students call him Jim or Jimmy, said it was the pedagogical difference between *teaching* and *fostering* and he preferred to foster.

Katie, she had a little class. A respect for authority. He kept thinking that he should Google her name from home to see if she kept a blog, see if maybe she was harboring a small crush on him. Who could blame her?

"Yes, Katie, I understand," he said. He liked the way her name sounded in his mouth. It helped that it was also his ex-wife's name, though that was just coincidence, he was sure. "That makes perfect sense. So why don't we do this. Everyone, take your quizzes home with you. Complete them at your leisure and bring them back, and all of you will get the grade you've earned."

That was enough for the Back Row of Fucktards, which meant it would be enough for the Good Students, since all the Good Students really wanted in life was to be like the Back Row of Fucktards, the kinds of people who managed to pass their classes without any mental exertion at all. The whole school was filled with future middle managers anyway, Cooperman thought. It really was no use being like Katie Williard. Ten years from now, someone from the Back Row of Fucktards would be her boss regardless.

Cooperman felt absurd pulling up to the Sonic in his white-on-white Escalade, but it was important to convey a positive image while doing business. It was the rap music he had to blast out of his speakers that really bothered him, particularly now that it was 2:44 and there was no sign of his business associate, which made the fact that there was a middle-aged white guy dressed like a professor sitting by himself listening to The Game all the more obvious.

It was all that bitch and ho shit he couldn't stand—he'd grown up on LL Cool J and Run-DMC, even liked Public Enemy despite their anti-Semitism and Farrakhan crap, always sort of thought Chuck D had his head wired for revolution, could have been like Martin Luther King Jr. if he hadn't been saddled with that clown Flava Flav. The big joke was all that drug hustling rap music. They even had a media class at Fullerton on the subject; it was called Street Documentary: The Socio-Economic Impact of Rap Music, and every semester kids lined up to get in, as if that class would ever save the goddamned world from itself.

Anyway, he only listened to gangsta rap now so that he could figure out what the hell people were saying to him, both in class and on the streets, and so guys like Bongo Fuentes, who was now officially late for their appointment, wouldn't think he was a complete asshole.

It wasn't supposed to be this way. Fresh out of graduate school, Cooperman got a top-shelf research job working for Rain Dove, the sprinkler industry equivalent of being drafted in the first round by the Dallas Cowboys. Within a year he was the big dog in the Research & Development department, but by his fifth year on the job he was thinking about even bigger possibilities. The sprinkler industry had always been about making the world green, about giving customers the impression that no matter where they happened to live, they were in lush surroundings; that their backyard could look like the eighteenth hole at Augusta if only they purchased the latest automatic sprinkler system. It was a successful model—one only had to visit Rain Dove's corporate offices in the middle of the Sonoran Desert of Phoenix for tangible proof.

Nevertheless, Cooperman saw the future one night while watching a Steven Seagal movie, the one were Seagal plays an eco-warrior who, after breaking fifty wrists over the course of a two-hour period, makes an impassioned speech to save the world from the disasters of human consumption. As far as epiphanies went, Cooperman recognized that this was one he'd probably have to keep to himself, but what he realized while watching Seagal pontificate was that change was coming—that if even marginal action heroes were taking time out of their gore-fests to admonish the very people they entertained to conserve, hell, it was only a matter of time before the offices of Rain Dove would be picketed by some fringe water-conservation terrorist cell or, worse, Seagal himself. Better to be ahead of the curve than be the curve itself.

He spent the next two years developing new technology that would actually *limit* the need for the expansive sprinkler systems Rain Dove was famous for. He migrated Doppler technology into existing systems to measure air moisture and barometric pressure, developed a probe that would constantly measure soil dampness, linked it all to a master program that calculated exact field capacity reports which would then decide, without any human interaction whatsoever, when exactly the sprinklers needed to go on. Or if they ever needed to go on.

And that was the rub. Test market after test market determined that most people who were buying Rain Dove systems actually lived in places that needed absolutely no irrigation at all. Grass would grow and die in precisely the manner it had since the beginning of time, with or without a system, and specifically without Cooperman's vaunted RD-2001.

At the time, he had a huge house in the Sunny Hills neighborhood of Fullerton (the locals called it Pill Hill because of all the doctors who took up residence there); he and his now-ex, Katie, were talking about having kids (which meant he'd have to cut down on his weed smoking, since their doctor said it was lowering his sperm count to dangerous levels) and seriously considering a little condo in Maui. Still, he always had the strange sense that he was living in the opening shot of a Spielberg movie, right before the aliens showed up to turn the bucolic to shit.

He shouldn't have been surprised, then, a week after the last test market showed everyone just how cataclysmic the RD-2001 would be to the sprinkler industry, to find himself out of a job. But that was his problem. He was like one of his goddamned students, never thinking about ramifications, never watching the ripples, even when his own fear system kept setting off alarms.

A month later, he was out of a wife.

A year, he was living in his parents' house in Buena Park and making pro–con lists about his life, trying to figure the relative value of killing himself.

Two years and he was using the RD-2001 technology to grow some of the most powerful weed in the universe.

Three years, he was supplying.

Cooperman checked his watch again. It was now 2:55 and The Game was pledging allegiance to the Bloods though suggesting even Crips could enjoy his rhymes. Where the fuck was Bongo? In the years they'd been doing business, Bongo had never been late for anything; in fact, Cooperman couldn't remember showing up to a meeting and not finding Bongo already impatiently shifting from foot to foot like a five-year-old needing to piss. Back in the day, when Cooperman just bought weed for his own consumption, Bongo was his connect. Now they were essentially partners, though he never really got the sense that Bongo liked him. They didn't have much in common, of course, apart from the weed, but they'd made each other a lot of money, and because of that they often shared moments of happiness together, which Cooperman thought gave their relationship a unique value.

At 3:00, Cooperman's cell phone rang, the opening strains of "Nuthin' But a 'G' Thang" replacing his preferred rotary dial ring tone. It was one of those songs that he thought would make him sound authentic if anyone he needed to impress happened to be nearby when the phone rang, but that was never the case. No one ever called William Cooperman because he usually didn't give anyone his number. Still, when he looked at the display screen and saw Bongo's digits he felt inordinately relieved.

"You had me worried," Cooperman said when he answered.

"You wanna tell me again what the fuck happened in Mexico?"

"I thought we were meeting."

"You at Sonic?"

"Yeah."

"Then we're meeting."

"This is bullshit, Bongo," Cooperman said.

"So was shooting a motherfucker in the face," Bongo said. "So now we're even."

The problem in dealing with criminals, Cooperman had learned, was that most of them were paranoid and narcissistic, which isn't an ideal combination. Everything was a personal affront. There were only so many ways of telling someone that you weren't going to fuck them and that you respected them completely, before you started to think of ways to fuck them and disrespect them just to change the conversation. Cooperman hadn't reached that level with Bongo yet, but he recognized that his problem in Mexico was probably a subconscious manifestation of that very thing. Since losing his job at Rain Dove, he'd read several books on leadership structures and realized that he was guilty of doing that very thing with his RD-2001. Made sense he'd do it again. But that didn't mean he wanted to lose this job, too.

"Listen, Bongo," Cooperman said, "it was completely my fault. I got nervous and everything fell apart super quick. But I want you to know that I'd never fuck you, and I completely respect you and your position."

"You shot a motherfucker who couldn't even read," Bongo said. "You realize that? You killed a motherfucking illiterate."

"The failure of education isn't my problem."

"You think this is funny?"

In fact, Cooperman did think it was funny, if only in the way everything seemed off kilter to him these days, as if each moment were separate from the next. He liked to think that he'd finally learned how to compartmentalize, finally got over his obsessive tendency to overanalyze all things, what Katie used to call his "ego-driven OCD." But the truth was that once he set something aside, he never even bothered to think of it again. Cooperman realized this likely meant he was losing his fucking mind, but even that got shoved aside in time. Like this Mexico shit. He'd driven down to Tijuana with a trunk full of his reconfigured RD-2001s to sell to a contact of Bongo's, who was then supposedly going to move them to some influential people in Nicaragua, who, if they liked the system, would bankroll an entire development program. Or at least that was the story. But when Cooperman finally met up with the contact—he was just a punk, really, maybe eighteen or nineteen, who didn't look all that different from the faux gangsters and frat boys who rolled across the Fullerton campus en route to their Freshman Comp sections—a switch flipped in Cooperman's head. He finally saw the ripples in their entirety: The Nicaraguans would take his technology, backwards engineer it, and he'd be out of a job in two months, maybe less. This adjunct teaching shit, which he only did so he could pay off his monthly alimony, would be his entire life. Teaching Intro to Goddamned Water to a whole legion of consumers who wouldn't change anything for the better, would just perpetuate the world's problems, so that in ten years, or twenty, when people were really staring at the end of things, they'd eventually ask who was responsible for teaching these morons how to conserve, and that's when fingers would start getting pointed at the educational complex and guess what? He'd be out of a job again anyway.

Cooperman ran it all through his mind from several different angles to make sure he wasn't overreacting, examined the empirical evidence, and then he shot the kid in the face.

It wasn't even like it had happened without Bongo's complicity, really. Bongo had asked Cooperman months before if he wanted a gun, since Cooperman refused to have any additional security at his house, apart from the rent-a-cops who worked the gate at the Coyote Hills Country Club, and since Cooperman thought the neighbors would find it odd that a bunch of gangsters were loitering around the community pool. So he said sure, absolutely, since it sounded like the type of thing he really should want, even if the idea of shooting a gun went against all of his previous political inclinations. Yet, once he had his handsome chrome-plated nine, Cooperman started going to the Orange County Indoor Range in Brea to shoot, and found he rather liked unloading into the bodies of the various people who'd done him wrong over the years, at least metaphorically. The problem was that Cooperman wasn't much on metaphors, and after a while he started thinking about making a trip out to Rain Dove's corporate offices in Phoenix to discuss further his anger regarding his termination. It wasn't like he wanted to kill anyone, specifically, only that whenever he left the range he felt positively Republican for the first time in his life. Like the kind of guy who handled his problems versus having his problems handle him.

So when the switch flipped, Cooperman did what those leadership structure books always advocated: he *rightsized* his problem.

Crazy thing, it felt pretty good. Taking the power back. All that.

"I admit my mistake, Bongo. What do you want me to do? The kid shouldn't have stepped to me. You know me. I don't G like that."

Cooperman heard Bongo sigh. It wasn't a good sound. He'd already sketched out for Bongo a general idea of how things had gone down in Mexico the day previous, substituting the moment of self-realization for a hazy recounting of the kid waving a knife in his face and trying to steal his car. He knew when he told Bongo the story the first time that it was filled with holes, so he tried to cover his tracks by saying things like, "And I'd never seen so much blood!" and "I can't sleep now, Bongo, I keep seeing that knife blade in my face!" and "It was all slow motion. One minute, we were sitting there in the Focus, the next he was jabbing a knife at me. What was I supposed to do?" Cooperman thought his mania would make Bongo realize he'd been really scarred by the event, since it wasn't every day Cooperman killed somebody, and that it was therefore only reasonable things weren't lining up correctly.

"All you had to do was hand him a couple fucking boxes. That's it. No reason for you to feel threatened in the least. It wasn't even *illegal*. And this is what you do? You make some shit up about a knife?" Bongo said. "That kid had parents, Dog. Relatives. Motherfucker had an existence, you know? That shit went over five fucking borders. You think the Nicaraguans are going to just let that shit slide?"

"I highly doubt Sandinista death squads are coming for me," Cooperman said, but as soon as he said it, he began to think of it as a real possibility. "This is Orange County."

"You think that matters?"

"This is America!"

"Dog, this is what it is. Place don't matter in the least."

"I'm just a scientist," Cooperman said.

Bongo sighed again. It was an especially pitiful noise coming from him. He was one of those Mexican guys who looked like he had some Samoan in him, his torso like a barrel, his hair always shaved close, though sometimes he grew a rat tail off the back of his head, which he then braided. He had a tattoo of his own name on his stomach, which Cooperman thought he must have gotten in prison, though he didn't even know if Bongo had done any time, but who would be bored enough on the outside to get that done? Funny thing, though, was that Bongo was actually pretty easygoing. Married to a woman named Lupe, whose face he had tatted up on his forearm. A kid. Coached soccer. One time Cooperman even saw him at the Rockin' Taco eating with his family, and they just nodded at each other. He had some hard knocks in his employ, there was no doubt about that, but Cooperman always admired Bongo's approach to business—apart from the timing issue—which boiled down to the simple credo tattooed in Old English on the back of his thick neck: *Not To Be Played.*

"I left what I owe you in the bathroom, second stall, taped inside the toilet tank," Bongo said. "I can get you twenty-four hours to get ghost. After that, I don't know you."

"That's not going to work," Cooperman said. "I've got a job. I've got a life here. I can't just get ghost. Let's be reasonable. Bongo? Bongo?" Cooperman pulled his phone from his ear to see if he'd lost the signal, but it was still four bars strong. He called Bongo back, but the phone just rang and rang, didn't even go to voicemail.

"Well, fuck you then," Cooperman said and set the phone down on the passenger seat. Thinking: *I'll just let it keep ringing. See how annoyed that makes him. Let him know I'm not just going to lie down. William Cooperman doesn't get played, either.*

Cooperman reached under his seat for his nine, shoved it into the front pocket of his Dockers and got out of his Escalade. He circled around the Sonic once to make sure there wasn't a SWAT team waiting for him, and then entered the restroom. The only person inside was a Sonic carhop, still in his roller skates, washing his hands at the sink. The only sound was the running water and the constant ringing of a cell phone, which sounded like it was coming from inside the second stall.

"Oh," the carhop said when he saw Cooperman. "What's up, teach?"

Cooperman looked at the carhop, tried to see his face, but he was finding it hard to concentrate on anything. Bongo had been right fucking here, the entire time; probably got off watching him stew in the front seat of his car, probably thought about killing Cooperman himself. Probably should have. Christ.

"Who are you?" Cooperman said.

"Ronnie Key?" He said it like a question, like he wasn't sure that was his own name. "I'm in your Intro class."

"Where do you sit?"

"In the back," Ronnie said. "I know, it's stupid. I should sit up front. All the studies say people who sit in the front do better, but, you know how it is when you have friends in class, right?"

"Right," Cooperman said. The longer he looked at Ronnie, the less he seemed real, the less the words he said made any sense. Maybe it was that constantly ringing phone that was making everything skew oddly. Maybe it was that he could feel his nine pulling the front of his pants down, making him aware that he looked like one of those slouch-panted thugs he avoided at the mall. "Was there a big fucking Mexican in here a minute ago?"

"I'm not sure."

"There is no 'not sure,' Ronnie. Either a human being meeting the description of a big fucking Mexican was in here or was not in here."

"Professor, I'm not sure I know what you're talking about."

*Professor.* Of all the times to finally show some deference. It never failed to amaze Cooperman how often people could astonish you, because even the way Ronnie had said the word indicated a kind of awestruck reverence for the moment, for all the time Cooperman had put into his place of academic standing, even if the truth was that he'd put in shit for academics, it was all just the sprinklers that had brought them to this shared moment. Or maybe it was just confusion Cooperman heard. Either was fine with him.

Cooperman stared at Ronnie Key for a moment and tried to decide what to do next. His options seemed simple enough. Shoot him or let him roller skate back into his mundane life. The realization that those were his two best choices sealed the deal.

"I have to take a shit," Cooperman said. He walked over to the second stall, opened the door and closed it behind him, then waited until he heard Ronnie skate out the door before he dropped Bongo's ringing phone into the toilet. The cash was right where Bongo said it would be, but there wasn't much there. Maybe ten thousand. Enough to get out of town, but then what?

This whole thing was ridiculous. At his house in the Coyote Hills Country Club, where he'd lived a grand total of six months, he had another fifty, maybe more, plus his entire harvest growing in his backyard, which would net three times that much this month. Probably closer to four. He wasn't a big mover. Cooperman had no delusions about that, he was just happy to provide a niche market, so maybe he'd been wrong ever thinking globally with this whole Nicaragua thing in the first place; but he'd realized that in time, that was the ironic thing now.

Cooperman just wanted to go home, spark up a bowl, grade some papers, and forget this mess, but going home didn't seem all that prudent. He realized Bongo was trying to do him a favor, realized that Bongo could have killed him if he wanted to, could have alleviated this now-international incident without a problem, but didn't. Cooperman didn't know what to make of that precisely, except that perhaps Bongo felt a level of loyalty. Another surprise. Getting out of town was a gift from Bongo, but where would he go? He'd lived his entire fucked up life in Orange County, and it's not like moving to Palm Springs was going to somehow change the end result that a bunch of angry Nicaraguans were now looking for him.

He stepped out of the stall and saw that the sink where Ronnie Key had been standing not five minutes before was now overflowing with water, the tile surrounding the sink a growing lake of piss-colored water. His natural inclination was to turn the faucet off and conserve the water, but then he thought about where he was standing; thought about how just up the street there used to be groves of orange trees that grew wild from the water in the soil that had, nevertheless, been ripped up and paved over; thought about the chimpanzee and gorilla that lived in a cage next to that weird jungle restaurant on Raymond back when he was a kid and how no one seemed to give a shit that it wasn't in the least bit natural; thought about how nothing in this place has ever lasted, how it's always been a course of destruction and concrete gentrification. And what did that produce? Nothing came out looking any better, Cooperman thought. No one had figured out a way to make the Marriott across the street from campus as pretty as the citrus trees that once lived in the same spot. No, Cooperman decided as he walked back out into the furnace of the late afternoon, the faucet still going strong behind him, no one ever recognized the ripples.

The indignity of teaching adjunct at Cal State Fullerton extended beyond the known quantities of indignant students and the horror of keeping a clock. On top of it all, William Cooperman, who'd invented the most technologically advanced piece of sprinkler machinery ever, who thought he should be held up as a paragon of conservation and awareness in this new "go green" world, who'd figured out how to grow marijuana in an environmentally sound way that actually heightened the effectiveness of the THC in ways that could probably help a lot of cancer patients (and in fact, that was what Cooperman had always thought he'd use as his alibi when he was finally busted, that he was growing a mountain of weed in his backyard as a public service to those poor souls with inoperable tumors and such), "*the* William Cooperman," as his ex used to call him, had to share an office.

It was up on the second floor of McCarthy Hall and overlooked the Quad. During the term, it wasn't such a bad view. Cooperman even sort of liked sitting at his desk and watching the students milling back and forth. As long as he didn't have to teach the students, he actually rather liked the idea of them, of their determination to learn, their collegial enthusiasm for stupid things like baseball and basketball tournaments, their silly hunger strikes protesting fee hikes, the way every few years MEChA would demand that California be recognized as "Occupied Mexico" even while they happily wore Cal State Fullerton T-shirts and caps. Back in the 1970s, riot police beat the shit out of students in that Quad, but now things were much more civil. Protest was just as cyclical as the tides and, in a bizarre way, it comforted Cooperman during the school year. It also made the prospect of sharing his space with *fostering* Professor James Kochel less offensive since there was something to occupy his vision other than Kochel's collection of "family" photos, all of which were of cocker spaniels, and shots of the geology professor in various biblical locales.

In the summer, however, it was just the two of them with no view to speak of, since the students who liked to protest and march and rally in the Quad typically avoided summer session. Cooperman didn't know where they went and didn't really care normally, but the loneliness of the campus this evening made him nervous as he walked from the faculty parking lot to McCarthy. He paused in the Quad and looked up the length of the building to see if his office light was on, and sure enough he could see Kochel moving about. Cooperman found it strangely comforting, especially since he'd left his gun in the car, figuring he'd just run upstairs, grab his laptop, maybe heist a few other laptops from open offices since they'd be easy to sell along the way to wherever, and then . . . *get ghost*. Bringing a gun onto the campus might awaken his worst traits, a likely scenario since he was supposed to be teaching another class within the hour, and that meant a few students might show up early wanting to *talk*.

He harbored a fantasy, momentarily, that when he got to his office Katie Williard would be waiting for him and he'd grab her, too, and they'd run off and start a life. Tend the rabbits together, Cooperman thought, and realized the sheer folly of it all, but that's what fantasizing was for.

Anyway, he hadn't figured out where, precisely, he was going, but had a vague notion that the Pacific Northwest would be a hospitable place for the world's finest weed grower, even sort of liked the idea of finding himself in a place like Eugene or Olympia or Longview or Kelso, particularly since he'd spent the last few hours liquidating his bank accounts and now had forty thousand dollars in cash stowed in the Escalade, a couple RD-2001s, and, finally, a reason to leave. The idea of living in near constant rain had a sudden and visceral appeal, and it astonished Cooperman that he hadn't thought of living in Oregon or Washington previously. He liked apples as much as oranges.

Cooperman climbed the two flights of stairs up to his office. He was surprised by how light he felt, how clarity had lessened the weight he felt about all of this crap. It wasn't just about water anymore; it was about living a more principled life. He'd stood for one thing for a very long time and what had it earned him? Cash, of course, but in the end no one cared that he possessed the key to saving the world. What good was it being a superhero if no one respected your superpowers?

Proof was right in front of him, even: Professor Kochel's name plate was above his on the little slider beside their office door. Respect was dead, so fuck it to death. Maybe I'll get that inked on my neck in Old English, Cooperman thought. Fuck it to Death.

"There you are," Kochel said when Cooperman finally opened the office door.

"Have you been looking for me?"

"Your phone has been ringing constantly. I took some messages for you." Kochel handed Cooperman a stack of Post-it notes. The first was from Katie Williard, another was from Enterprise Rent-A-Car—a problem Cooperman hadn't quite taken care of yet—and another still that had one word on it: Bongo.

"What did Katie Williard want?"

"Lovely girl, isn't she? So bright."

"What did she want?" Cooperman heard a new tone entering his voice. He liked it. Thought it made him sound like the kind of guy who just might have some neck ink.

"Candidly? I think she's upset about your afternoon class."

"Did you talk to her?"

"Briefly. She indicated to me that she just wasn't satisfied in the level of teaching. It's no reflection on you, William, I'm sure."

"I'm sure."

"I've had Katie in other courses and she's just very particular," Kochel said. He had a look of smug satisfaction on his face that Cooperman recognized as the same face he used when he talked about how his faith in Christ allowed him to see that many of the great mysteries of science were merely God's way of testing us.

"Someone named Bongo called?"

"Oh, yes, sorry," Kochel said. "That's what the name sounded like. I could barely hear him."

"He say anything?"

"It was very strange," Kochel said. "I thought maybe it was a wrong number. All he said was to tell you that he couldn't get you twenty-four anymore. I have no idea what that means. Do you?"

Cooperman looked out the window and down at the Quad, half expected to see an army of men already massed. But it was empty save for a lost seagull picking through an overflowing trash can. It was still sunny out, would be for another hour and a half, two hours, not that it probably mattered. The more frightening aspect was that Cooperman couldn't remember ever giving Bongo his office phone number.

This was not good.

"No," Cooperman said. "Must have been a wrong number."

"Anyway," Kochel said, "you should really ask for voicemail in the fall."

"I won't be here," Cooperman said. He was still looking out the window, but wasn't sure precisely what he was hoping to find. Something or someone that seemed out of place. Like a guy walking around with a MAC-10. Across the Quad, a black SUV pulled up in front of

Pollack Library. A man holding a stack of paper walked out of the Performing Arts Center. A gust of wind through the breezeway picked up a Starbucks cup from the ground. What he wouldn't give for the Quad to suddenly fill with riot police.

"No?"

"I've been offered a job back in the sprinkler industry," Cooperman said.

"It really is a despicable profession, if you must know," Kochel said. "From a geological and religious standpoint, if you must know."

"Who must know anything?" Cooperman said.

Kochel started listing the people who must know things, starting with the media and the Muslims and all of the impressionable students who were being led to believe that science was the one true God. The Starbucks cup hovered in the air and then fell and then was swooped up again in another gust. Wind technology. Maybe that's where he'd make his second wave.

"What time did this Bongo call?" Cooperman asked when Kochel eventually ran out of righteous steam.

"Now who must know something?"

Cooperman turned from the window and found Kochel staring at him in beatific glory. Why had he left his gun in the car? A dumb mistake, really. But he wasn't used to being the kind of person who was always packing, at least not on campus. "What fucking time, Professor Kochel," Cooperman said, his voice finding an even deeper register than before, "did this fucking message come in?"

"Ten minutes ago," Kochel said. "Okay? Ten minutes ago."

"Thank you," Cooperman said. He fixed his gaze back out the window. A man got out of the backseat of the SUV in front of Pollack and walked in a semicircle, a cell phone pressed to his ear. Cooperman couldn't make out his age or his exact race from his vantage point, but could see just from watching his body language that the guy was confused about something. It was probably nothing.

"If you want my opinion," Kochel said, as if Cooperman had just asked him a question, "you might want to look into anger management courses. Your attitude in a corporate environment will be a real detriment. Not everyone is as easygoing as I am. You get back with a bunch of MBAs and those egos, well, I'm just saying it might be a bad fit."

The man from the car was walking toward McCarthy now, his cell phone in his hand. He looked like his head was on a swivel—looking this way, that way, back behind him—and when Cooperman looked back up at the library, the SUV was gone.

"I'll work on that," Cooperman said.

"I know this isn't your speed, Will, but you might also start thinking about your relationship with the Lord."

"That sounds like a good idea," Cooperman said. The man was in the middle of the Quad now, and Cooperman could finally make him out more completely. He was older—maybe fifty—and wore white slacks and a black shirt, had on wraparound black sunglasses, nice shoes. Cooperman thought he was maybe Mexican, but couldn't really tell. He tried to think if he knew the difference between a Nicaraguan and a Mexican, at least in terms of appearance, and once again cursed himself for having lived in Orange County all of his life.

It didn't really matter, anyway. Cooperman was getting the fuck out while he still could. He grabbed his laptop, a few books that meant something to him—*Forest Hydrology* and *Groundwater Hydrology*—and, just in case, the Post-it with Katie Williard's phone number. Maybe once things settled down . . . well, it never hurt to have options with shared interests. He tucked everything into his messenger bag while keeping an eye out the window. The man was on the move again now, his pace more brisk, his direction absolutely clear.

"And anyway," Kochel was saying, and Cooperman realized his office mate hadn't ever stopped talking, was actually quite animated about something, "what you might find out is that everything has consequences, Will."

Cooperman turned to Kochel and studied him seriously. He didn't hate Kochel, didn't even really think about him on a regular basis, though he never enjoyed being around him. It wasn't even the religion that bothered him. It was the presumption Kochel had that he was always right. "You know, this is all very fascinating. I'd like to learn even more about this, James. Can we continue this conversation after I get back from my car?"

Kochel brightened. "Of course, of course, I'll be right here."

Cooperman took one last look outside before he exited his office, saw that the man was now only twenty yards or so from the building, and closing fast.

Professor William Cooperman stepped out of his office and closed the door lightly behind him. No panic, no fear in the least, just a person skipping out of his office briefly, just a person, just anyone at all. He looked down the hallway and saw that a few students were loitering down by the vending machines, another couple were lined up in front of the photocopier, two were sitting on the floor in front of his classroom reading from their textbooks. None of them bothered to look back at Cooperman, so they didn't notice him slipping Professor James Kochel's nameplate out of the slider and into his messenger bag, though Cooperman did pause for just a moment before exiting out the back of the building, to look at his own name. He liked how it looked on the slider by itself, thought that it looked esteemed and powerful and worthy of intense respect.

# Acknowledgments

I am indebted to the steadfast dedication and unwavering vision of my fabulous editors Gina Frangello & Stacy Bierlein and for their hard work on these stories. They ask me to take big chances and they don't let me fail. Additionally, I am ever thankful to Lois Hauselman for publishing me in *Other Voices* over a decade ago – I am so honored to continue the journal's singular tradition in these pages. Extra special thanks to Steve Gillis, Dan Wickett, Steven Seighman and the entire extended Dzanc family for bringing me into the fold and treating this book with such dignity and to Allison Parker for correcting my copious mistakes.

So many people have played a role in these stories, whether they know it or not: Jennie Dunham, agent, friend and confidante; Lee Goldberg, Karen Dinino and Linda Woods, siblings foremost, but also fellow travelers in this literary world and a constant source of love and inspiration, and my mother Jan Curran for giving all four of us the passion for writing; Lynne Sharon Schwartz for opening my eyes again; Tom Filer for still being the voice in my ear; booksellers Lita Weissman, Jan Valerio, Linda Brown, Bobby McCue and Maryelizabeth Hart for continually championing my work; Jay Ray for inspiring "Palm Springs"; Michelle Harding for teaching me how to direct an MFA program . . . and for not getting too angry when I left early to do this job; the staff and faculty of the UCR-Palm Desert Graduate Center and the UCLA Extension Writers' Program; my classmates in the Bennington Writing Seminars; my fabulous graduate students for understanding why they got their papers back so late; and, finally, my wife Wendy, who has so many words of her own to write, but who reads each of mine.

These stories originally appeared, often in significantly different form, in the following publications: "The Salt" in *Two Letters;* "Mitzvah" in *Las Vegas Noir;* "Walls" in *Barrelhouse;* "Palm Springs" in *Hot Metal Bridge;* "Living Room" in *Silent Voices;* "The Models" in *Santa Monica Review;* "Granite City" (as "Where The Ends Meet") in *Indy Men's Magazine;* "Will" (as "Lines") in *Hobart.*